DUST OF MY WINGS

A DANTE'S CIRCLE NOVEL

CARRIE ANN RYAN

Dust of My Wings
A Dante's Circle Novel
By: Carrie Ann Ryan

© 2014 Carrie Ann Ryan
ISBN: 978-1-947007-64-2
Cover Art by Charity Hendry

For more information, please join Carrie Ann Ryan's <u>MAILING LIST</u>.
To interact with Carrie Ann Ryan, you can join her <u>FAN CLUB.</u>

DUST OF MY WINGS

Lily Banner has spent her entire life oblivious to the true secrets of the paranormal world around her. When her day job in the lab puts her in the middle of a supernatural war bubbling just beneath the surface, she finds herself in need of help—but the aid comes from a stranger with more secrets than she could possibly imagine.

Angelic warrior Shade Griffin is charged with protecting the ancient secrets of the paranormals. But when he finds Lily, his world shifts, and his allegiance changes, forcing those who want Lily eliminated to take action.

The war between the realms is on the edge of a blade, and only Shade and Lily can stop it.

To Rebecca Royce. Thank you for the plot bunny that bred even more bunnies. You are amazing. I love you.

ACKNOWLEDGMENTS

Thank you oh husband of mine for dealing with my grouchy moods when I had a tough time. Thanks for dealing with our kittens Miley and Maxie, and thank you for getting me a new "office" chair. I love you.

And finally, thank you to my readers. I am so blessed with you guys. You guys are amazing. The emails, Facebook comments, tweets, and notes make my day. It's because of you that I get to do this.

Thank you.

CHAPTER 1

A summons from the council never led to good things. Shade Griffin's millennia worth of experience told him that. No matter what he truly desired, he'd do what he was told. He didn't have another option, and why would he disobey now? He never had before. Whatever demands they dealt might seem tedious to a long-lived being such as him, he didn't have anything else better to do.

Such was the life of an angel in his predicament; a vast and endless sense of being, yet no one with whom to share it.

Shade shook off the misery that threatened to creep along his skin and suffocate him. The idea of sharing his endless life with someone else, someone special, had long since burned away. No need to think about it again.

The sun broke through the clouds, warming his cool, honey-colored, almost dark tan, skin. He lifted his face, letting the rays soak into his pores. His eyes closed, and he took a deep breath, not really wanting to leave the spot. He rolled his neck, stretching his muscles, and then opened his eyes. His back ached from the long flight to the enclave. He stretched his wings, the light shimmering off his midnight black wings that trailed to a rim of deep blue. The wind picked up, his blue-black hair flowing behind him.

Shade arched his back, his wings flared, and blue dust trickled off and into the air, and drifted to the ground below.

Damn stuff kept doing that; and there was nothing he could do about it. He clenched his fists and winced in pain. He looked down at the healing abrasions on his knuckles and muttered a curse.

As one of the appointed enforcers of angelic law, he'd just come back from the punishment of a young angel: a cocky one at that. He hated doing it, but the unrepentant jerk had decided it would be fun to fly in broad daylight without cloud cover over Area 51. Really? Cliché much? It was easy enough to downplay the event as another UFO sighting, which would certainly bring out the crazies, but it didn't negate the fact that the reckless angel had broken angelic law by letting humans see him flying.

Because he had decided to laugh about it to his friends and merely shrugged it off, Shade had to step in. If he'd apologized, then Shade wouldn't have had to use his fists. But no. The young one mouthed off and challenged him, so Shade had to accept. After all, as a warrior, he could not ignore a challenge. Doing so would negate his authority.

And he won.

Of course.

He still hated punishing others, even though it was his job. Between him and his best friend, Ambrose, who was practically his brother, they dealt with most of the enforcing the angelic laws. Together they'd done what they had to do for centuries, and in Ambrose's case, even longer.

Shade was a warrior angel. In the times of the Angelic Wars, he'd fought alongside the best of the best. Hell, he was the best of the best. Well, maybe tied with Ambrose, but he wouldn't tell the other angel that.

Shade chuckled as he envisioned Ambrose's reaction to his thought. Ambrose was sure to want to prove just the opposite to be the case, and Shade would be more than willing to give it a go. *If you couldn't fight for supremacy with your best friend, how else would you even know how good you were?*

Now those wars were long since over. Times of awkward peace were at hand, meaning the warriors herded the other angels and made sure they followed the rules the council members set in place.

They followed the rules, even if the rules were sometimes, in his opinion, too strict for their own good. But he would never voice it. He was merely a warrior angel.

He wasn't even a godly one like in the fables of mortals. Their race wasn't that of a god. Yes, if theology was correct, a god at some point had created them, but they weren't God's right hand men; they were not the symbol of goodness and hope. Far from it. They were just another species with rules, regulations, and a seemingly endless long life in order to be subjugated.

Wow. Bitter much?

He shouldn't be; he had everything he wanted, didn't he? His forehead scrunched as he thought, and his wings fluttered a bit in agitation.

He certainly had all the money, titles, glory, and privileges a warrior of the finest caliber could have. Why did he feel like he was missing something?

Shade shook his head and looked around. He stood at a midpoint on the mountainside, the enclave circling him. Stone buildings jutted from rock faces, thousands of feet above the surface, old as time. No stairs or elevators here. Open the door and, without wings, they'd drop to their death. Marble and crystal twinkled in the sunlight from the adornments and windows on all of the structures. It may have looked cold to some, but to Shade and his angelic brethren it was warm and inviting.

It looked like home, but it wasn't truly a 'home'; There was no love waiting on the other side of the door, and that pained him.

He sighed. He really needed to stop thinking such depressing thoughts. Taking one last look at the place he called home, he jumped off the ledge, his wings spreading to catch a drift, as the cool breezes hit his skin. He flew past other angels in the air, nodding to a few, but kept to himself. He was a warrior angel, the last face some would see as they stared beyond the end of his blade. Tough to make life-long friends outside of certain circles that way.

Shade descended, the wind whipping his hair back from his face, until his feet touched the stone balcony set off the council chambers. He set his wings back, making sure they didn't trail on the floor. He was exhausted, but that didn't give him a reason to be lazy. He walked through the ornate doors that reached tall to the roof. Despite his thousand years of living, sometimes the immense beauty of the council chambers had him at a loss for words.

Gold and crystal adorned the walls. Intricate carvings and art filled the room. Eons of pride and talent gave the room a sense of grandeur and honor that made Shade feel young in relation to the other angels surrounding him.

In reality, he was the youngest warrior angel of them all, and second in command to Ambrose, the leader of the warriors, the best at the job. That wasn't pride talking, just fact.

Shade walked to the center of the room and surveyed the five council members before him, perched high on their thrones, their noses turned up towards him. Another presence worried him. Ambrose stood off to the side, a frown on his face. What was happening?

"I see you have finally decided to grace us with your presence," Caine, the leader and all-around pain-in-the ass, admonished, and Shade held in a scowl. The brown-haired angel lifted a lip as if the mere sight of him disgusted the ruler.

Shade bowed his head. "I'm sorry I was late. I had just finished my dealing with the young angel and needed time to clear my head before I came. I didn't want to taint the council with the thoughts and actions of a warrior." There. That didn't sound like sarcasm and distain, did it? Well, maybe it did, but it was the best he could do. He wasn't overly happy with Ambrose in the council chamber. It felt like an ambush.

Caine snorted and shook his head.

Okay, apparently he couldn't quite mask his true feelings. Oh, well.

Shade didn't hate the council. He just didn't like the fact that they held all the power and didn't seem to do anything but hand out decrees and punishments that were enforced by the warriors. There were only three classes of angles: the council, the warriors, and the others. He didn't like all the power on the top that trickled down to nothing, but who was he to speak out of turn?

"Enough of your pleasantries. We need you here, now," Striker, the second-in-command, cut in. Dishwater brown hair and plain features made him look almost human. If it weren't for the brown wings coming out of his back, he'd look like a mortal. Maybe that's why the angel was always an ass.

"Okay." Shade nodded. "What is it that you need?" He once again wondered why Ambrose was there? Why did they need two warrior angels? Tingles of dread filled his belly. Had the other faction of angels done something? They hadn't destroyed the rebels completely in the war. It was always a cause for trepidation and concern that the others would come back and start something. Were they on the brink of another war? He'd not heard anything, but he couldn't be too sure.

"We have been alerted to a breach of security," Caine announced. "Our secrets may be unraveled soon if this is not fixed."

"You mean the secrets of the supernatural?" Shade asked. "How can that be?"

Striker gave a laugh, filled with bile rather than humor. "You dare ask this when it is your fault we are in this predicament in the first place?"

Shade froze. "What?"

"Your dust." Striker sneered. "Your oh-so-favorable blue dust has been collected by a human. If it falls into the wrong hands, do you understand what will happen? Everything that has been held secret for eons will be lost because you have a dusting problem."

Oh, crap.

As a child, he'd had a problem with his dust. Whenever he got excited or angry, he'd sprinkle dust where he flew or stood. Beyond a few occurrences recently, he'd thought he'd conquered it years ago. How had someone gotten it? Did they even know what it was?

"I didn't know," Shade whispered.

But that was a lie. He did know. Just that morning, he'd seen a sprinkle of his dust flowing on the wind and thought nothing of it.

My God. What have I done?

"We know you didn't," said Agnes, the sole female

member of the council. Her piercing blue eyes filled with understanding.

Of all the council members, Shade liked her best.

"But," Agnes continued, "you must fix it, Shade. Finish it. Find your dust and reclaim it before someone finds out what it is. We don't have the power to wipe the memories of an incidence such as this from a human's mind as we once did. The humans don't believe anymore. Because they don't, we've lost our ability to shield ourselves the way we should."

Shade nodded, sadness and frustration setting root.

"I will fix this," Shade promised. "You have my word."

The council nodded and dismissed him. With a glance toward Ambrose, Shade left the room, his best friend on his heels.

The two friends didn't speak once they reached the end of the balcony. They simply jumped off the edge, their wings catching the wind, and flew toward another mountaintop. Shade needed time to think. To calculate.

He was damned fine at his job. Strong and fierce. Yet a childhood problem of dusting could take down a civilization. He would have laughed at the ridiculousness of that statement if it hadn't been true.

They landed, their feet settling on the soil. Shade looked behind him at the place he called home. They didn't live in heaven because they weren't godly angels, far from it. He wasn't even sure there was a heaven beyond their time. Their world was in the same realm as the humans, but it was tucked away in a pocket of space between two mountain ranges, hidden from the eyes of the unknown.

A few raindrops fell from the sky before turning to a slight mist. The other angels who were at a lower altitude flew to the safety of their homes, the rain beginning to weigh heavy on their wings. Only the strongest could fly in anything more than mist, another reason they didn't live on clouds, as most humans seemed to believe. One flight through a dense cloud could be dangerous; the moisture seeped into their feathers and threatened to drag the angel down. Without sufficient muscular back strength, the angel would plummet.

Most didn't. Despite the vast strength they possessed, angels were weak in some respects.

"Are you going to stand there in the rain and watch others while everything falls around you, or are you going to fix this?" Ambrose's deep voice cut through his thoughts, and Shade turned toward him.

Tall with white blond hair pulled back from his pale face in a braid, with white, almost crystal wings, Ambrose was the light to Shade's dark. Yet, the colors masked the personality, for where Shade saw the humor and light in some things, his best friend was the dark, the edge to the blade. Shade, too, held his own fury; he just didn't show it as often.

Dangerous and agile, his mentor had taught him everything he knew. Shade lowered his head in shame. He'd failed.

"You didn't fail, Shade," Ambrose whispered.

"I didn't say that aloud." Ambrose was always doing that. He was practically a mind reader

"You didn't have to. We all leave trails of angel dust. You

are no different from others except that you leave greater quantities. It's not something to be shameful of."

"I beg to differ."

"It's only different this time because it got into the hands of a human. I'm worried how it got there, which is why I was in the room when you came in."

Intrigued, Shade lifted his head. "What are you saying?"

Ambrose shrugged. "I don't know yet. Something just seems off to me, but I will work on finding out."

"Okay, what else do you know?"

"Only that the dust may be in the hands of a woman."

"A woman?" Interesting.

THE MOTORCYCLE VIBRATED BENEATH SHADE AS HE PULLED off the side of the road and parked. The rain pelted him, the cold seeping into his bones, but he shrugged it off. He was in northern Washington, and this seemed to be the norm in terms of weather.

He lifted his leg and got off the bike, ignoring the stares of the women around him. They watched him stroll, his powerful legs leading to long strides. He'd tucked his wings into the slits in his back to hide the fact he was an angel, but he couldn't hide his face or the fact that women seemed to fawn over it.

It had been a long time since he had a woman, not since that jaguar shifter a century or two before on a night of deep depression and loneliness. But the heat, claws, and desperation had served to fill only a physical need that left him even lonelier than before. From that moment on, he left his carnal needs up to his hand. Before the jaguar, it had been even longer, but he didn't want to think about her. The one he'd lost. She was long since gone.

Shade walked into a nearby café, the smells of baked goods and coffee filling his nose. He ordered a small coffee then went back to sit at a table near the window so he could watch those who passed by. A male pixie, in human form, walked in front of the window and nodded toward him. There were so many supernatural beings hidden from view in the world that Shade couldn't even count them.

All humans were diluted forms of supernaturals. For millennia, the supernaturals had bred with one another and mixed the species until, finally, their powers had dwindled in most, and they stopped believing in things that came out of fairy tales. Those with so little non-human blood running their veins that they seemed ordinary were now called humans, although each had at least something beyond human lying dormant in their DNA.

Council did not identify the name of the human who collected the dust, but Ambrose told Shade it was about to be in the hands of a woman who lived and worked nearby. Her name was Lily.

Who was this Lily? Shade wanted to get a look at her. She had the answers. She possessed the reason behind his shame: his blue dust.

A woman with expressive emerald-green eyes passed by the window; a slight smile graced her face, and she had those side-swoopy bangs women loved so much. She was of average height and held delicious curves. He looked over every inch of her—a small waist, large, perfect breasts to fit his palms, slightly wide hips that would serve well when he gripped them, and sexy legs beneath the hem of her brown coat…

Lily.

That had to be her. He didn't know how he knew, but he was sure of it.

His groin tightened.

She was human. Not a lick of anything else came from her. Yet, why did he want her so from just a look? He'd never looked at a human this way before. Why now? Was it because she might be the one who held his dust?

Lily stopped under the awning right in front of the window, careful of where she stepped—*odd*—and brushed the hair out of her eyes, before smiling at a passerby. She was radiant. Absolutely gorgeous. Shade held back a groan and shifted uncomfortably in his seat when she bit into her lip. She smiled again then walked to what must have been her car, got in, and left before Shade even thought to stand.

Some warrior he was, completely frozen in shock by his reaction to her. He was, however, unrepentant. He didn't want to follow her today anyway. A town small as this would know of Lily and aide him in his research. If the supernaturals were revealed, chaos would rain. Humans could feel threatened, start wars, do untold atrocities when they met with what they didn't know and therefore feared. If the supernaturals felt threatened…Shade didn't want to think about that. He had to know more before he did anything.

So many questions flashed through his mind. Who was she? Why did she have his dust? What would she do if she discovered his secret?

Most importantly, he wondered if she was single and how she would look underneath him, blushing in ecstasy.

Shade shook his head, dispelling those annoying thoughts. He'd find out what he needed to about Lily, get his dust, and save the entirety of the supernatural world. Maybe along the way he'd learn a little more about a pretty brunette whose very presence threatened to make his wings stretch to the sky.

Yep. Easy for a warrior angel such as himself.

CHAPTER 2

Lily Banner hated her job. Hated it. There was nothing worse than being on the bottom of the totem pole and knowing there was nowhere to go but down. Was that even possible?

She blew her bangs from her face in frustration. It was late in the day, way past her usual time off. She desperately wanted to go home, but work was never ending. Every day seemed to drag a little bit more of her soul out of her body. God, she hated her job, and it wasn't as if the work she did meant anything. She had a chemistry degree, but she didn't do anything with it. Not being at the top of the class, she really couldn't have gone on to graduate school and made anything of herself. Frankly, she had no interest in pursuing higher education. School had been a chore, and it made her feel like she was nothing. So, now she was just a lab tech at a soils testing lab for a company she hated. For a boss she hated.

Oh, yeah. For a man. Lily rolled her eyes and held back a snort. Why on earth had she changed her life for a man, particularly for a man like Bryce? Wasn't she supposed to be a strong new age woman? Apparently, not so much.

Bryce, her ex-fiancé, was a cheating asshat. He now lived with Miss Fake Boobs and their three bratty kids.

Lily sighed. Whatever. She was over the whole thing. She really was.

She straightened the stack of folders on her desk for the third time. They just couldn't get straight enough. Though the lab was clean, it still didn't feel clean enough for her. Still, she organized everything on her desk at precise angles, and there wasn't a lick of dust on any surface around her. That was workable.

Her entire system had been blown several days before. It still irked her.

"Lily, I have something for you." Her boss, Glenn, had strode to her desk, his permanent smirk on his face. At the age of forty-three, his body looked a decade older with thinning hair and an increasing waist. He always smelled of sweat and greasy burritos.

He wanted her and wasn't afraid to make it known.

She'd held back a shudder as she always had at the errant thought of those greasy hands groping her.

Not in this lifetime. Or the next.

"Do a run on this." He'd thrown a sealed, clear pack containing a vial on her desk.

She'd winced as it hit the wood hardtop, leaving a line she'd have to clean later. The plastic knocked her stack of papers askew, and she quickly picked up the package and ordered her desk again. God, how she hated that man. About as much as she hated messes.

"Sure, I can do that. What type do you want on it?" She'd picked it up and peered through the plastic. The vials contained some kind of blue dust, but she couldn't really determine anymore than that just from a site analysis. "Do you want a liquid or solid?"

"Don't alter it. No liquid, just a solid."

Lily had nodded. That made sense. If they didn't know what it was, there was no use trying to dissolve the sample in a solvent and cause a reaction, because, if she tried to do that, it might destroy it or cause an explosion. "I'll do a proton and maybe a carbon on it then. The 400 will be open soon once I spin down the current sample, and I can to the proton first." The proton NMR was the easiest one to do and would help identify what was in it.

Glenn had waved away her words. "Fine, fine. Whatever. Just get it done. ASAP." He turned on his heel and walked away without another word.

The nerve of the guy. Didn't he know it wasn't a simple plug and chug system? That she had to go through tons of work before she could even set up the probe? Then when she got the results, she had to go through the analysis to see if the peaks could tell her something about the composition of the sample and what exactly was in it. Lily shook her head. Of course he didn't know. When was the last time he'd done anything concerning chemistry?

Regular work, however, had taken precedence, and now, several days later, Lily was finally getting around to analyzing the substance. That is, if she had time before she had to leave.

She grabbed the package and walked to the lab. She opened it and took out the vial then went about cataloguing it into the system. Now that she could get a closer look, she held it to her eyes. Were those flecks of silver and black in the blue? What the heck was this stuff? It didn't look like chalk and there wasn't much out there in terms of silicates and ceramics that were naturally blue. Maybe it was a synthetic. That would make her job that much harder since it then would be a man-made substance and really difficult to figure out.

She shrugged. No use in worrying too much about it now. She spun down the sample currently in the NMR, saved the data to the backup hard drive, and shut down the system. With a quick look at the clock, she cursed because she was running late. Well, late for her. She still had time, but she always liked to be early. She walked back to her desk and locked the new sample in her desk. Any work would have to wait until tomorrow, or else she knew she'd be stuck in the lab until after midnight for sure. She'd just get it done tomorrow.

Lily blew the hair from her eyes and bit her lip. She hated putting things off for the next day *again*, but there wasn't really a choice. Glenn wanted things done immediately. He didn't understand that each run took hours. She wanted to leave now, but she still had a couple more things to do. With a sigh, she sat back down at her desk and re-opened a program file she'd been working on and began an analysis of a previous sample. It seemed never ending.

At twenty-seven, she'd never thought she'd be where she was. She always thought she'd be married with children at this point in her life, but that wasn't a possibility considering she couldn't remember the last time she had a date. She wasn't ugly; she knew that, but, apparently, she wasn't suited to anyone's taste. Her medium-length, chestnut brown-hair had natural highlights, and she'd just trimmed the swoopy bangs she loved so much. Her pale skin didn't have many freckles since she was such a homebody. As a kid, she'd been afraid of sunburns. She wasn't skinny, but she wasn't overweight either. Just a nice average woman with curves.

That was what she was. Average. Average looks, average intelligence and an average life. She wanted something more. Something, anything, to fight back the loneliness. Sure, she had a family, if you could call it that. There was a dad she never talked to and who was on a second honeymoon with his fourth wife. He said he was trying to rekindle the magic, but everyone involved knew it was only a matter of time before that faded away and he found Mrs. Number Five. She had a mom who was more passive-aggressive than the mom from the television sitcom *Everybody Loves Raymond. She* liked to belittle Lily and her choices every time she had a chance. But, other than that, Lily was alone.

No, that wasn't true. She had her non-blood family: her six girlfriends. They were her family of choice. They were seven women of different ages and professions who came together at least once a week to celebrate their lives, even if sometimes there didn't seem to be much to celebrate. They'd all met at their favorite bar, Dante's Circle, over the years and ended up being best friends. In fact, she was meeting them tonight, so she had to get moving.

"Hey, Lily, why are you still here?" Thad, the other lab tech on her floor, came up and hitched a hip on her desk. She held her breath but didn't say anything as he moved her pens. His eyes widened, and he moved back then straightened them.

"Sorry about that. I know how you get," he teased.

She flushed and shook her head. "It's fine. Really. I hate being a dork."

"You're not a dork. You just like order. Nothing wrong with that." He smiled, and his face lit up as if he wanted something.

Oh, no.

"So, Lily, you want to go grab a bite to eat tonight?"

She looked up at the younger man and tried not to groan. His dishwater-brown hair fell in his eyes like those skater boys, and he still hadn't filled out his lanky body with muscle. He was only working here before he went off to graduate school. At twenty-one, he still had his life ahead of him. She felt old and worn out, and not at all interested in a romantic relationship with him.

"Sorry, Thad, I can't. I'm meeting the girls for drinks, but thanks anyway. Maybe another time." Or never.

Disappointment filled his eyes, but he kept a smile on his face.

Oh, God, I've just kicked a puppy.

"It's okay. I understand. Well, I'm on my way out. Make sure you don't stay too late. I don't like you being here all alone. Do you want me to wait for you and walk you to your car?"

He was just so cute. In that 'little brother' way.

Lily shook her head. "I won't be long, so you don't need to wait for me. I'll be fine. I promise. I have my whistle and pepper spray." The town was relatively safe, but it never hurt to be prepared.

Thad grinned and tilted his head. "Okay, then. If you don't really need me. Good night, and be safe. Have fun with the girls."

"Thanks. Have a good night."

With a wave, he walked out, and Lily shook her head. He really was kind of cute, but not for her, and way too young.

Lily glanced at the clock again. Okay, she had about twenty minutes before she really had to go. She didn't have time to go home to change, so what she had on would have to suffice. It was just a drink with the girls. Something she desperately needed.

Her fingers flying across the keyboard, she worked at fitting peaks and labeling what she could. Before she knew it, her twenty minutes were up, and her head hurt. She really needed that drink. Sighing, she shut down her computer and packed up her purse. She straightened everything one last time and made sure her drawers were locked. With one last thought to that odd blue dust—*if not tomorrow, then Monday, for sure*—she shrugged and walked to her car.

Outside the wind howled and rain began to fall as thunder rumbled in the distance. Oh, great, a storm. She brushed her bangs out of her face. Should she just go home? Was being out tonight worth the aggravation? Her back ached and her head throbbed, and a bubble bath sounded divine. But, after her lonely thoughts during the day, she really needed to be with her friends. Decision made, she ran through the rain and unlocked her car door. Once inside, she shivered and turned the car and heater on to warm herself.

Yep. She really needed that drink…and maybe a dark, handsome stranger.

A giggle escaped, and she shook her head. Well, maybe just that drink.

Striker paced in his room. Shade had been gone for two days after the human woman. The warrior hadn't reached the council for updates or help as of yet, and Striker was getting annoyed.

With a huff, he turned again, his brown wings dragging on the floor. He hated the damn things. They were boring.

Average. Angels of every caliber had better-looking wings than him, but he at least held the power where most didn't. Other than his fellow council members, he was in charge, and if enough things went his way, and if his plan stayed on track, then he would be above the other members soon.

That thought brought an ease in his shoulders, and the tension he'd held since the dark warrior angel had walked into the council chambers faded away. He hated being relegated to a group of leaders. He wanted all the power. He wanted to rise above his average looks and reign supreme, and he would.

He'd been close—so close—before. Once, long ago, during the Angelic Wars. He'd led his armies and reveled in it, though that part of his past remained in secrecy. He couldn't let the other angels know that he'd been the masked angel behind the greatest army that spread fear and instigated rebellion. No, that wouldn't do at all. The current council—*sans* him—had fought and used their warrior angels to bring down Striker's army. But that had been a calculated move on his part; at least that's what he told himself. He let his second-in-command take the fall. The other angel had lost his wings—and his head—for the act.

Striker shrugged. At least it hadn't been him. This time, instead of an all-out war of opposing forces, he'd take over from the inside. The other council members were old, unaccustomed to fighting in these times of peace. Even though angels were immortal, age did matter. As time passed, they became stuck in their ways and refused to embrace new things. With their experience came selfishness and haughtiness. They were the easy ones to mold and bend to his will.

It was the warriors who created the problem for him. Shade and Ambrose, in particular. Ambrose was older than he was and would be hard to take down. Angels' powers increased as they aged, a fact that pissed Striker off to no end. No matter how far he progressed, the bastard went even farther. Ambrose did have one large weakness—his protégé and best friend, Shade. Luckily, Shade had a more immediate problem involving his dust. Shade needed to clean up his mess or risk exposing the supernatural. If he were to fail, then the warrior would lose his wings, and he'd be out of Striker's way when the time came. If Striker worked it right, then Ambrose's need to help his friend would lead to his downfall, as well.

Striker laughed and wrung his hands. Yes. This would all work. It had to work. He just had to make sure the human woman figured out something was wrong with the dust, and exposed everything that was hidden. Striker would rule them all with an iron fist one way or another, but would she find it fast enough? He might have to intervene. That was what he did best. After all, he was the one who'd given the greasy human male, the woman's boss, the dust in the first place.

Once the warriors failed, Striker would have his opening, and he'd finally get what he deserved after he lost it in the Angelic Wars. Power.

CHAPTER 3

Lightning sparked the night sky, and a heavy wind shook Lily's car as she drove to the bar after she went home to change. She hadn't planned on stopping to change what she was wearing, but she'd been soaked to the bone. After finding a cute top, pants, and calf-boots at home, and of course making sure everything was tidy, she'd scrambled back to her car and hurried to the bar. Cleaning up hadn't been for something like bringing a man back or anything. Lily snorted. She might be lonely, but not that lonely. Now she was running late. She hated running late.

Her windshield wipers slapped against the glass, and she squinted to see. The rain came down in sheets, but the town had enough streetlights that it was safe enough to drive at night. Her house was located in the lower middle class area of town that merged with the not-so-nice area where Dante's Circle was about five minutes away.

She loved the city. It was a smaller one, but not so small that everyone knew everyone else's business, but not so big that she felt lost in the shuffle, even though sometimes she felt just that. Luckily, she had her friends to help her.

She pulled up to the bar and parked under the awning that Dante had added a few years before to keep everyone dry. Since it always seemed to rain in their town, it was needed. She noticed that her friends' cars were already there.

Darn it. Her chest tightened as anxiety filled her. Being late wasn't like her. Early was on time; being on time was late. Showing up over forty-five minutes late was painful. She turned off the car and grabbed her purse and her phone.

Six missed calls.

Aww. They were worried about me.

That should tell her something—either that her being late was an oddity, or that they really loved her. Probably both. Stupid work. Stupid boss. Stupid samples. She really needed that drink and to decompress with her friends.

Lily got out of the car and walked under the awning, careful not to step on any cracks in the pavement. Some might call her weird, but those were her quirks and she could live with them. Her friends might tease her about them, but they loved her for who she was. If only she could find a man to do the same.

She sighed. What was with her tonight? Lonely much?

When she opened the door and took a step inside, she smiled and sighed. Oh, how she loved this place. Dark cherry wood paneling on the bottom of the walls darkened the room, but the light cream paint on the top made it feel homey. Mirrors, framed photographs and pictures, and assorted knickknacks covered the upper part of the walls. Despite the fact it looked slightly cluttered, it fit the atmosphere.

A pool table stood off to the right where a group of drool-worthy men played. They didn't look up when she walked in, and she tried not to let that hurt her. It wasn't as if she dressed provocatively or anything, but it would be nice to have someone ogle her just once in a while.

Really? *Get a grip, Lily.*

Dark wood tables with mismatched chairs were positioned randomly on the floor. Though her fingers itched to re-organize everything, this wasn't her bar so she'd let it be. The large wooden bar stood in the back with its original Irish taps and mirror sent over the pond years before by the Dante family, or so he'd said.

Her usual table sat in the back corner on the way to the kitchen and bathrooms, but it was directly across from the bar and was the only large round table in the place. Her girlfriends were already sitting there, their drinks of choice in their hands.

"It's about time you got here," Dante said with a wink when he saw her enter. Built like a Mack truck, the man was damn sexy. He had broad shoulders, a trim waist, and arms that man would envy. Women fawned over him, but he never gave them a second look. He just smiled and poured their drinks. He had long blue hair with black streaks, that was currently in a ponytail, and tribal tattoos running down his arms—and maybe other places. Small black hoops hung in his ears, along with a smaller hoop in his right eyebrow, and he had a tongue ring that gave most women shivers. But not her—he was just a friend. A hot friend, but not one she'd ever date. Becca, one of her other friends and Dante's bartender, often wondered if he had other piercings, but Lily was too afraid to ask him.

"Sorry, Dante." Lily smiled and blew her bangs from her face. "Work ran late, and the weather sucks out there."

"You want the usual?"

"That sounds great." Oh, how she needed that drink.

Dante poured her an apricot wheat draft and slid it across the bar. She loved when he did that.

"Thank you, Dante."

"No problem. Now go see those girls of yours. They were worried about you." He looked over her shoulder at her group, and a look of longing passed over his face before he quickly blinked it away.

Did she imagine it?

"Lily! Get over here!" Eliana called. Her shaggy red hair falling in her face as she shook her head in Lily's direction. A new bandage on her arm caught Lily's attention. Eliana was an artistic welder who made the most beautiful metallic designs. Lily tilted her head in question, but the other woman just shook her head.

Okay, then.

"I'm sorry. Work caught up with me." Wow, she sounded pathetic.

"It's okay; we understand," Nadie said. "We were just worried about you." Nadie was the compassionate member of the group, a kindergarten teacher with soft, straight blond hair and vivid violet eyes that seemed to hide something beneath the sweetness.

"I saw the calls," Lily said. "Thanks, you guys."

"It's no problem," Jamie assured her. "It just wasn't like you. I see you have your beer. Tell us about work." Lily had always admired Jamie's striking looks. She had beautiful brown hair that framed her caramel-color face, but Lily knew she could never pull off the blunt bangs. She was the owner of a small bookstore where they sometimes hung out when not at the bar.

"Just the usual," Lily explained. "Too much work, not enough time. I hate my boss."

"That greasy man?" Faith asked. She ran her fingers through her black bob, leaving it in its perpetual state of disarray. Faith was their resident photographer and always had a camera on her or nearby. Lily looked down at the floor near Faith's feet, and saw the camera bag and she held back a smile.

"Yes, that greasy man." Lily sighed. "I don't understand how he can *always* smell like burritos. I'm sure he eats other things. Come on!"

The women broke out in laughter and took another sip of their drinks.

"Another round, Dante!" Amara called out, waving her arm. Her auburn curls danced around her pale face. Her eyes looked tired, and it was no wonder. She was the manager of the local inn, and she attended business school at night. She hoped one day to start a business of her own. Tonight was one of the rare times she didn't have to work.

"Okay, ladies, but only one more since you are all driving," Dante answered. "Becca? Do you think you can get those? I need to go change out one of the kegs."

Becca gave a dramatic sigh and rolled her big green eyes. "Fine, but don't think I'll do anymore. This is my night off."

Dante gave a dramatic bow, his long, blue ponytail brushing the floor. "Of course, my lady. I shall ever be in your servitude."

"That sounds about right." Becca chuckled, then tripped on her way to the bar. "Damn new shoes," she mumbled.

"Or, it could be your two left feet, doll," Faith called out.

Becca flipped her off and went behind the bar.

"Hey," Lily objected. "Be nice. She's about to get your drink. Just think of what she could do." She visibly shuddered. She didn't normally like going out to eat since she couldn't be sure of the cleanliness and germs, but she trusted Dante to keep the place clean.

"Too true," Nadie added. "I'm going to go up and help her. Should I add in our normal food orders? Appetizers?"

Everyone agreed, and Nadie skipped off to help Becca.

"So, I told you about my lovely boss," Lily said. "Now, tell me about your days."

"Not too much," Jamie answered. "We got a new shipment of western romance novels. I already have most of them on my Kindle, but I like having some of them in paperback anyway." She shrugged. Though the rise of ebooks hurt her business somewhat, she'd taken a chance on a venture and had added a small café in the inn that attracted many loyal customers. She also hosted in-house events that invited patrons to gather and share their book recommendations with others.

Some bought them there or went home and bought it online. Either way, she made money, and Lily was proud of her.

"I had a shoot today with an uppity bitch, but it was okay," Faith added. "I'd rather have been down the block taking pictures of kids playing on the playground, but those don't bring in any cash." Faith could bring inner beauty and soul out of anyone she photographed; or she could capture the nitty-gritty and not-so-beautiful that lurked beneath the surface. She was truly a talented artist.

"We had about four cancellations today that annoyed the hell out of me," Amara complained. "The linens were late so we didn't have table cloths for the first thirty minutes of the brunch. Of course, our owner decided at that moment to visit, but I think I took care of it. I'm just happy that I don't have classes this week, and I got a head in my work, so I can actually try and enjoy myself tonight."

"What about you, Eliana?" Lily asked, afraid of the other woman's answer because of the bandage on her arm.

Eliana frowned and took the last drink of her beer. "Not much. This piece is just pissing me off, and the damn paper boy scared the hell out of me, so I burned myself." She held up her hand as the others tried to soothe her. "I'm fine. Really. It's not that bad. It just itches like a bitch."

"Okay, we have drinks," Becca interrupted, a tray full of appetizers in one hand and Nadie behind her with chips and salsa. "Dante will bring out the rest of the food when it's ready. He can get off his lazy ass and take care of it. I'm off."

"I heard that," Dante called from the back.

Becca rolled her eyes. She scooped a large dollop of salsa on a chip and shoved it in her mouth.

"You should be nicer to him," Nadie admonished. "He does a lot around here."

"You just think he's cute," Becca said with a snort and nearly choked. She waved her hands in the air indicating she'd be okay. She took a big gulp of her drink and smiled.

Nadie blushed, and Lily reached across the table and squeezed her hand. Nadie's crush on Dante was a well-known fact in their group. Not that the quiet woman would ever act on it. She gave shyness a whole new meaning.

"You know, you should just ask him out," Faith said. "I mean, what could go wrong?"

"Shh! Oh, I don't know." Nadie bowed her head and didn't look at anyone. "He could say 'no' and then kick us out for annoying him, and then we couldn't be friends anymore."

"That's ridiculous," Lily countered. "You're beautiful and sweet. Any man would be lucky to have you." It was true, but that didn't make her feel any better about her own loneliness. She shook her head, not wanting to think of that anymore. "Let's talk about something else."

"Okay," Jamie agreed. "Like what? We already talked about jobs, and apparently, the topic of men is off the table."

"You know, doing it on the table is quite nice," Becca added.

Lily choked on her beer. On a table? "Really?" Wait. Why did she ask that?

Becca raised a brow. "Come on, sweet Lily. Don't tell me you've never tried it."

She blushed and shook her head. Was there another way to do it other than with the lights off and missionary?

"I thought we were going to talk about something else," Lily mumbled.

Eliana sighed. "Like what? The weather?"

Dante set down their food and left before they could even thank him. *Such an odd man.*

"Well," Jamie said. "It is storming out there harder than usual. I'm surprised we all got here like we did. I had expected that some of us wouldn't want to drive."

Lily shuddered, a tingling feeling running up her spine. "I know what you mean. I was even later than I would have been because I needed to go home and change. I got soaked just walking from my office to my car. In fact, we should probably call it a night soon, just in case the weather gets worse."

Everyone nodded, drank from their waters instead, and finished their food as they talked about work and guys. The other patrons filed out as they finished their drinks, so it was only Lily, her friends and Dante left in the bar. No matter how some of them tried to steer their conversation away from the topic of men, they were seven single women after all. Seven single women. Of course they talked about guys and sex. Oh, how she missed sex, even the boring kind she used to have. Maybe with that dark-haired imaginary stranger who kept coming to mind. Oh, yes, someone she didn't know and who didn't know about her craziness. Since she was imagining a man anyway, he'd have broad shoulders, caramel skin and would taste like chocolate. Oh, yes, and she'd run her tongue up his abs and maybe down to his—

"Lily," Jamie called out, bringing Lily out of her sex-driven thoughts.

"Yes?" Blood rushed to her cheeks. Did they know what she'd been thinking? From Becca's raised brow, just maybe.

"Do you want to go to the park tomorrow afternoon and play dominos again if it's dry?" Jamie continued. "I'll have time off, and we haven't been down there together in ages."

One of her horribly kept secrets in life was her dominos addiction. There was just something about using numbers to align pieces in a precise order that got her blood pumping and her competitive edge going crazy. She used to play with her maternal grandfather before he'd passed so long ago. Now she couldn't stop playing. She'd go down to the park, play dominos with her grandfather's friends and enjoy herself. Maybe that explained why she couldn't get a man.

"I'd love to. Hopefully, this weather will clear up soon."

Someone opened the front door to the bar, and a gust of wind knocked over a chair, startling everyone.

"What—" Lily stood up to see what was wrong when another gust of wind knocked her back. The lights flickered, and the building shook. Out of the corner of her eye, she saw Dante run into the room and cover Nadie with his body as the glass windows shattered and a bolt of lightning struck the room. Not a piece of furniture…but *the room*.

The bar stood silent in an eerie glow, and time seemed to stop. The bolt of lightning branched out with spindly fingers, its tips reaching Lily and her friends directly in the chest. Lily's body tingled and her hair stood on end. The lightning bolt ran through her system, sending her into a state of shock. She heard someone scream, and Lily struggled to breathe. Her friends stood around her in the same state. She turned to reach for Jamie's hand, but the lightning intensified, causing her to fly across the room and she landed with a thud on the floor. Her body convulsed and darkness pulled her under as Dante roared into the night.

SHADE PULLED HIS BIKE OVER TO THE SIDE OF THE ROAD AND ripped off his helmet. His hair flew on the wind as the rain pelted him.

What the hell was that?

The road had felt like it had turned into a roller coaster, and a bolt of lightning—an electric shock —had shot through the town. He'd lived through countless storms, natural and paranormal. He'd never felt anything like that.

He looked around, but from what he could tell, nobody came out of their homes to see what had happened. He shrugged and put his helmet back on. He'd continue on his way home, and if he passed anyone who needed help, he'd stop. There wasn't anything he could do now short of driving all over the city searching for the power source.

He pulled up to the small house he'd rented for the duration of his assignment, opened the garage, and pulled in. As he got off the bike, Ambrose rushed out, a scowl on his face.

"Did you feel that?" he asked. His blond hair had come loose from its band, something highly unusual for his stern friend, and it flowed around him.

"Yeah, all the way across town. Do you know what it was?"

Ambrose shook his head. "No, I've never felt anything like it."

Shade's eyes widened. If someone as ancient as Ambrose was confused, then it might have never happened before. That was downright scary as hell.

"Well, that doesn't sound good. What are you doing here? I thought you were out searching for something." Shade put his helmet away and led the other angel into the living room.

The house was a nice fit for a bachelor, but not so much for two people; Ambrose was staying with him. But they made it work. The place came furnished with brown couches and rugs with the typical standard fare of Target art and decorations. It suited his purpose just fine since he didn't plan to stay that long, though if he had any time off, he might do the landlords a favor and fix up the backyard some. In his free time, he liked to create rock formations and landscape structures. His home at the enclave had acres of rocks and waterfall formations that he'd created from granite. He did all the labor, and it gave him an outlet for the fury and darkness that threatened to override his otherwise calm demeanor; a fury he hid so well from others.

"I came to tell you a bit more about this Lily of yours," Ambrose answered.

"She's not my Lily," Shade said, then he realized he'd said it a little too rushed.

Ambrose merely lifted a brow. "Touchy. I see you've met her then."

He shook his head. "I've only seen her through a glass window. I didn't speak to her." But, oh, how he wanted to meet her, and then maybe bend her over the coffee counter or spread her over the table to see if she tasted like strawberries. He didn't know why, but she looked like she'd taste like strawberries. Ripe, sweet strawberries...

Ambrose gave him a blank stare.

Oh, shit. Had he said that aloud?

"So." Shade cleared his throat. "What else did you find out?"

Like is she single?

Really? That was what he was thinking? The entire world might go up in flames because of his dust, and he couldn't get his mind off a woman with big green eyes. Frustrated with himself, he cursed, then went to the fridge for a beer.

He pulled one out for himself and handed another beer to Ambrose.

"I don't want to know what you're thinking, but I will

say it's okay to think about another woman." His tone grew somber. "It's been long enough. You've mourned enough."

"That's funny coming from you. If you didn't want to know what I was thinking, why did you even bring it up?" His chest hurt at the thought of Ilianya and Cora. He shook it off. He didn't need to think about them now.

Ambrose sighed and took a long pull of his beer. "The woman works at an environmental research facility as a lab tech."

Shade froze. "Shit."

"Pretty much."

"What are the odds?"

"Exactly."

"So, I need to get the dust now, but if I do it without her knowing, then they'll notice it's missing. I mean, we could just take it and ignore the consequences. If they've already done analysis on it…it could be a problem." Shit, this had just gotten even more complicated.

Ambrose nodded. "I don't think we can simply go in and take it. You're going to have to sway her into giving it to you."

"What do you mean?"

"Woo her, do something. I already know you want her. Use that."

Anger coursed through him. "You want me to use that woman? Who are you?"

Ambrose's expression turned to stone. "I'm someone who lost everything in the last wars, and I don't plan to let anyone else lose their everything. Don't you understand?

We don't know what she knows. We don't know who else has the results, or even if she has the results at all. The thing is, the dust won't just come up as an unknown substance. It'll be worse. It's not of this world. The lack of anything normal at all will raise a red flag. We don't have the luxury of letting that happen. Plus, the lore of our dust has always been entwined with the ability for humans to see magic. I don't know if that's true, but it's something that we can't risk. We don't know how the council knows about the dust. All of this reeks of something under-handed. So, use her. Find out what you can, and I will find out what the council knows because something is going on under the surface of this, and I need your head in the game."

Shade just stood there. "I know something's off about this assignment. I don't think I can use a human like that."

"You just think she has a pretty face."

"You're a cold, unemotional ass."

"I became what I had to when Ilianya died and I lost everything."

Shade flinched at the sound of his dead sister's name; a name that neither of them spoke aloud very often. Angels may not age, but they could die. Painfully. They could heal most wounds…but not all. "Don't push me, Shade. This isn't a time for hurt feelings. You need to make nice with that woman and find out what you need to. This is bigger than her, bigger than us."

"I'll find out what I have to and get my dust. I won't use her unless I have to. I don't want to hurt her." He hadn't even spoken to her, but he already felt a connection with this Lily. Damned if he knew why.

His friend let out a breath that sounded as old as Ambrose. "I know you hate this. I do, too, but it's our job. We must protect our secrets no matter what."

Shade shook his head and finished his beer. "It doesn't mean I have to like it."

"Sometimes I wish all of our problems could be fixed with a sharp blade rather than a lie." As a weapons enthusiast, that was a saying the older angel loved.

"Come on, let's get some sleep if you're staying here. I have a guest room. In the morning, we can get to work on the council and Lily, and maybe find out what the hell that weird energy was."

"Sounds like a plan."

They walked to their rooms, and Shade sighed. Yeah, it was a plan, but in his heart, he knew it was the wrong one. He just couldn't think of a better solution without revealing who—and what—he was. That bugged him to no end because, frankly, he really wanted to get to know Lily and make her, as Ambrose put it, *his* Lily.

Lily's head ached, and her eyelids felt heavy. Her body still pulsated and tingled, and energy fluctuated through her limbs, shocking them before weighing them down like heavy sandbags. As she tried to move, her body revolted and shuddered. It was too hard to think. Her mind fizzed as if she'd had too much to drink. No, that wasn't right.

Memories from before she closed her eyes came to the front of her mind. A flash of light. A gust of wind. A scream.

Lightning.

Oh, God.

She shifted and her hand caught on something. A sharp sting shot up her arm. A trickle of warm, wet liquid trailed down her arm. Blood. Sensations slowly seeped into her body as the tingling numbness ebbed away. Her body ached as if she'd worked out too hard then thrown herself against a wall. Twice. With a groan, she wiggled her toes. Good. Not paralyzed then. She did the same to her fingers and sighed. At least she could feel them, pain and all. Small miracles. Gathering her strength, she cracked open her eyes, and quickly shut them again. Even the dim light of the room blinded her. Her head throbbed to a faster staccato. Fighting the urge to throw up, she opened her eyes again, slower this time. Her teeth bit into her lip, and she lifted her head and upper body.

From where she was, she could see tables were overturned, chairs stood on end and glass littered the floor. The dark cherry wood paneling had splintered off in some places, while deep crevasses and nicks took up the rest. The framed pictures had fallen off the wall and now lay on the floor, their glass broken; the smiling faces in the frames frozen and unaware of the scene around them.

Lily shook off the glass and tried to do the same to the blood that ran down her arm from small cuts and sat up fully. She turned her head, taking in more of her surroundings. A foot encased in a sensible, black Mary Jane caught her eye, and she gasped.

"Jamie?" *Please let her be all right.*

"I'm okay." Jamie sat up and brushed the debris from her clothes.

Lily looked her friend over and didn't see any blood or cuts, and she bit back a sob.

She stood up, wobbling a bit in her now not-so-cute boots, and looked around. The rest of her friends were conscious and sitting up. Relief flooded her. Becca leaned against a chair, her red curls in a tangle around her face. A large gash ran along her hairline, but the blood was only a small trickle. Amara sat underneath the bar by the stools, clutching her arm.

"Amara?" Lily croaked. "What's wrong with your arm?"

The other woman shook her head. "I just banged it against something, but it's not broken. That I would know."

Lily inwardly cringed. Of course, Amara would know what a broken bone felt like; she'd had enough of them growing up, but that wasn't something she really wanted to think about.

"H-holy cr-crap." Faith stuttered, her black bob in a complete disorder. She had a slight cut on her face. "What was that?"

"I have no idea," Dante answered, his face serious as he held Nadie close to him and gazed over her body, most likely checking for injuries. "Is everyone okay? Anyone hurt?"

Everyone shook their heads.

"Just cuts and bruises," Becca said, and winced as she tried to rotate her shoulder. "Okay, lots of bruises, but I don't think anything's broken."

Lily took a deep breath and surveyed the room. "How did this happen?"

Dante growled. "A freak storm. I'm going to call the paramedics; I want you girls to get looked at before you go." He looked down at Nadie, who uncharacteristically glared at him. Lily didn't know what was going on with the two of them, but her head hurt too much to worry about it.

"We're fine. I just want to go home," Eliana moaned.

"What if you have a concussion? All of you blacked out," Dante countered.

"We're fine. Really." Lily said.

"I don't care." Dante glowered at each of them in turn. "I'm calling 911, and you're all going to get looked at. I'm not taking any risks or no for an answer."

With a collective sigh, they all nodded. It was the smart thing to do anyway.

Lily rolled her neck and sat down on a stool that hadn't been broken, careful to avoid any splinters. "What about your bar? What can I do?" It wasn't the mess that bothered her, though on a normal day she'd scream at the disorder. No, it was the fact that Dante's pride and joy lay in a heap of broken chairs and clutter. How would he ever rebuild it the same way it was and still capture the essence that made her feel like she was at home? Yeah, he could try, but would it be the same?

Dante sighed and shook his head, walking away from Nadie, who continued to glare. "I'll think of something. After all, it's just stuff. The most important thing is that all of you are all right."

"Okay, but I want to help you clean it up," Lily offered. It was the least she could do.

Dante gave a small smile. "I knew you wouldn't be able to stand the mess too long, but, no, I'm okay."

Jamie hobbled to Lily's side and sat next to her with a huff. "So."

"So."

"Are we going to talk about the obvious thing?" Faith asked, a trace of fear woven in her normal snarky façade.

"What?" Lily asked. "Like the fact that the eight of us might have been struck by lightning and are alive to talk about it without any obvious serious injuries or burn marks?" Some of the fear from Faith's voice wrapped around Lily's heart and squeezed.

This wasn't normal. Seven women and one man living through a lightning strike with only a few cuts and bruises just couldn't happen. It was improbable boarding on impossible. Yet, here they were. Proof that odd things happened and with no explanations.

Faith gave a rough laugh. "Yeah, that."

"You're the scientist," Amara said, still clutching her arm. "This is weird, right?"

Lily swallowed hard and winced at the ache in her side. Did she lie to her friends to make them feel better or tell them the truth? The answer was easy.

"Weird, scary, and unheard of."

Her friends sat in silence, wide-eyed and still.

"Okay, what does that mean?" Becca asked.

"I don't know," Dante put in. "It's crazy, and anyone who hears us talk about this will say the same. They'll say we're certifiable, and those who do believe us will hound us for answers. The lightning that attacked and shocked us didn't do any real damage to us. Yes, we're banged up, but we should be dead."

She looked around at her friends and took a deep breath, careful of her bruises. "So, I suggest, if you want to keep your privacy and your sanity, keep the *shocking truth* to ourselves unless someone mentions it. Even then, I wouldn't say anything. I don't want you all to be hurt because of this. It might be better to come up with a story that it was just the strong wind that blew in the door and leave out the lightning."

Lie? Seriously? Maybe not a true lie, but a lie by omission. She was a scientist who craved order, stability, and solving the unknown. Deceit and fabrications weren't in her genetic make-up. Could she do it?

Lily looked around the room at her friends who, except for a few cuts and bruises, looked perfectly okay. No one would believe what had happened to them.

"Okay, Dante. I agree," she said.

One by one, her friends nodded in agreement, sealing their lie ready to hide the truth.

LILY WALKED INTO HER APARTMENT AND SET DOWN HER purse. She winced as she sat on her sofa and took off her once-cute boots; they were now covered in scrapes and dirt and were beyond redeemable. Darn. She'd really liked those boots.

She laid her head back, the soft cushions of the couch comforting her, and then she shot back up. What was she doing? She was filthy and spreading her dirt all over her clean house. With a gasp, she stood up, darted to the bathroom, and stripped out of her clothes. Once naked, she balled up the clothes and put them in her hamper.

Lily turned on her shower and let it run to let the water heat up. It always seemed to take forever. She tried to ignore the mess she'd left in the living room. It wouldn't do any good to run out there naked and start cleaning when she was cut up and dirty.

The paramedics had arrived just minutes after Lily and her friends had made a pact to keep the lightning event a secret. None of the women or Dante had any broken bones or signs of internal bleeding, so they were allowed to go home after a quick exam. They were advised to call 911 if they felt dizzy or anything, but since they'd all lied and didn't divulge the fact that they'd all lost consciousness, the paramedics were none the wiser. Dante had told the authorities that it was just a gust of wind and a strong storm. The officers seemed to take the explanation at face value and merely nodded then left, and that was that. Everything, on paper anyway, was normal; it had just been a freak windstorm that damaged a building and left some patrons with mild cuts and bruises.

Lily let out a breath and gripped the edge of the sink. Her body tingled from the energy flowing through her. She'd lied to the other girls. She didn't feel normal. She felt…

Well, Lily didn't know how she felt. Just weird.

She looked into the fogging mirror and hardly recognized herself. Her face was flushed and her eyes bright. Her chestnut hair was in a tangle.

What the hell had happened?

She shook her head. There wasn't anything she could do about it now. She needed to shower, clean up her mess, and then go to sleep. She was still going to meet Jamie in the morning to play dominos.

The hot spray felt soothing against her skin as she stepped into the shower stream. Though her body ached and she could have fallen into bed and never come out, she needed to go to the park tomorrow with Jamie. Playing gave her a release from the pressure that assaulted her throughout the week, a release she didn't get anywhere else.

Especially from a man.

The water trailed down her breasts, stomach and then pooled at her feet. She closed her eyes and moaned at the soreness that spread across her back and sides. She needed to relax. She closed her eyes, and images of a dark-haired stranger with strong hands assailed her. She imagined his hands replacing the water droplets and splayed across her skin. Her breath picked up as her stranger pulled her closer and pressed his mouth to hers. Her head rolled back as she imagined his hands working her nipples and then going lower. Her hand lowered to her mound of its own accord, and she touched herself, shocked at the heat. She rubbed her body against her hand and thought of her stranger's deep voice resonating naughty words that left chills on her skin.

Just as she was about to press herself closer into her hand, the water turned cold, and she gasped.

Darn it. She couldn't even get off in her mind.

She rinsed the last of the soap out of her hair and turned

off the water. She toweled off and then hobbled to her room. Once dressed in some comfy sweats and a tank, she went to the kitchen to get her cleaning supplies. It wasn't as if she could just *leave* the mess in the living room.

God. She really did need a life.

With a groan, she went back into the living room and cleaned up every speck of dirt and grime she might have left. Her friends said she had OCD and, frankly, she agreed with them, but she could still function in the real world with it. She just liked order.

Her muscles ached as she scrubbed out the last of the dirt and put everything away. Her house could probably use another deep cleaning, as it had been two weeks since she'd last done it, but she was too tired to think, let alone clean.

Like a zombie, she dragged herself to her room and pulled back her down comforter. She lay down, turned off her side table lamp, and closed her eyes. Though her body pulsated with an unfamiliar energy, she was just too tired to deal with it. Maybe in the morning things would make more sense. As she drifted off to sleep, an ice-blue-eyed stranger filled her thoughts, and she smiled.

Yes, he would be a perfect stranger to meet. If only he existed.

CHAPTER 5

Shade pulled his bike up to the curb at the park and turned it off, the vibrations still rumbling through his body. He loved his bike. It was like flying, just on wheels. He always felt so confined in a car, but with his bike, he felt free—like with his wings.

He took off his helmet and shook out his shoulder-length black hair. He'd almost tied it back but decided against it. The long locks could hide his face better if he were truly seeking out answers and didn't want to be remembered; people would remember the hair and not his face.

A human woman bumped into his side and smiled coyly. "Oh, I'm so sorry," she purred.

Shade didn't bother with a reply. He gave her a curt nod and lifted his gaze to look behind her in a dismissal. With an obvious pout, she huffed away. Good. He wasn't here to placate the feelings of a woman who didn't interest him. No, he was here for Lily. The file had said she liked to play dominos in the park on Saturday afternoons, and he wasn't going to waste an opportunity to meet the wide-eyed beauty.

He adjusted himself as his cock rose to attention just at the thought of her. He'd only seen her through the paned glass, yet he wanted her. He liked the way her average height held such delicious not-so-average curves. Those damn sexy hips of hers begged his hands to grip them as he rammed into her body bent over any surface he could find.

Shade groaned and pinched the bridge of his nose. This was *so* not the time to be thinking these thoughts. He'd seen the woman exactly *once* and didn't know a thing about her that he hadn't read from a file.

Oh, and the fact that she held the evidence that could destroy him and his brethren.

She couldn't be the woman for him, but he could still look. He just had to make sure he could still function.

A slight gust of cool air whipped through his hair, and he shook his head, thankful for the breeze that cleared his thoughts. He had a job to do, and that job didn't consist of fantasizing about a woman with big green eyes.

Since the freak storm the night before, the weather had cleared up to be a pleasantly warm day with a cool breeze to temper the heat. It was the perfect day to find Lily and gather any information he could. He hated that he had to resort to smiling and flirting to get what he wanted, but it might be the only way.

He walked through the park, his black boots making little sound on the concrete. He passed children playing on swing-sets, their mothers and fathers looking on in loving fashion, and, in some cases, boredom. He passed couples walking hand in hand, talking about their days and futures. Shade ignored the slight pain in his chest at the thought. He'd lost his happily-ever-after years ago and didn't need another.

He was only here for the woman, not for a trip down memory lane.

Shade continued through the park until he reached the tables and benches that ran along the opposite side of the park, where he stopped in his tracks.

There she was.

Lily sat on a bench alone, her legs pulled up, and her arms wrapped around her knees. A box of dominos lay on the table in front of her, unopened. She rested her pale cheek on her knees, and he could feel the tension riding through her from where he stood.

What had happened to her in the day since he'd last seen her?

She looked as if she were ready to burst at the seams with energy, yet looked jittery and exhausted at the same time. It didn't make any sense.

Where was her friend, this Jamie that Ambrose had said she met with to play Lily's favorite game—dominos —weekly?

Something was off, but he couldn't tell what from where he stood. She looked so lonely. Shade wanted to run to her and wrap his arms around her, never letting her go. He barely refrained from doing just that, but he couldn't just let her sit there alone with such a forlorn look on her face. He had been planning on making this just a reconnaissance trip, but plans had changed.

Taking a deep breath, he walked toward her. She looked up when he purposely used heavy steps to alert her of his presence. Her green eyes caught his with alarm. Her dark brown bangs shifted and covered her eyes and he had to fight the urge to brush them away from her face.

She shook her head, moving her bangs back into place, and opened her mouth to speak, but no sound came out.

Out of nowhere, energy swirled around them, sweeping though his body, and he almost had to sit down with the rush of adrenaline in his system. From the look in her eyes, he was glad she was already sitting down.

What the hell is that?

Shade cleared his throat and smiled. He heard an intake of breath, and she blinked rapidly. "Hello," he rasped. His body pulsated with energy, and he felt a connection snap into place with her. *Damn, what was going on?*

"Hello," he repeated. "I'm Shade." He held out his hand, and she awkwardly accepted. The feel of her soft hand in his calloused one almost made him come in his jeans.

"Hi," she said hesitantly. "I'm Lily. Can I help you with something?"

Shade smiled again. Oh, she could help him with something, but he didn't want to look like a lecher.

"I saw you without a partner and wondered if you wanted someone to play with."

"Oh." The blush that rose on her cheeks looked damned sexy. "Sure, I guess. My friend was supposed to meet me, but wasn't feeling too well. I had almost decided to leave and call it a day and now here you are."

Shade gestured to the seat across from her, and she gave a nod. He sat down and spread the dominos in front of them. They each picked their seven tiles and slid the rest to the side.

"I'm sorry to hear your friend is sick. Do you usually come here on Saturdays?"

Oh, great. Could he have sounded more like a stalker? Well, technically he was. Sort of, but it was for a job and it didn't count. Much.

Lily's eyes widened, and Shade backtracked. "Sorry, don't answer that." He gave a small laugh. "I was just trying to make small talk. Apparently, I'm not very good at it."

Lily smiled, and her face lit up. "No, it's okay. I come here most weekends to play with my friend, Jamie, or with anyone who wants to show up."

Shade had the highest doubles, sixes, and placed the tile in the center. Lily blew her bangs out of her face, chose a tile, and placed it perpendicular to his.

"When did you start playing dominos?" Shade asked then placed a tile on hers.

Lily cocked her head, considering her next move. "When I was younger, it was the only game my grandfather would play. We used to play for hours, and he never let me win.

After many losses and hits to my pride, I finally beat him." She gave a wistful smile. "I loved playing with him."

"Past tense?" Shade didn't know why he was pressuring her on her past; he needed to know her present for his job, but for some odd reason, he wanted—no, needed—to know more about her past, present, and future.

"He passed away a few years ago." Lily didn't look up and played another tile.

"I'm sorry." He hated to see the sadness emanating from her face and posture. Why did he have to ask such a personal question?

Lily looked up and gave him a smile. "It's okay. It was a long time ago." She picked up a tile from the boneyard and placed it on their board.

"I'm sorry for bringing it up anyway. Tell me about yourself." He trailed his finger along the side of the cool tile before making his move.

"I'm quite boring, I promise you."

"Tell me something anyway." He needed to know more about her. Anything. That bothered him to no end. She might have pretty green eyes and a body that made him drool, but he didn't need to be thinking about who she was beyond his physical attraction to her. He was most likely going to have to hurt her in the end, if and when she found out the truth. He didn't want to make it any worse than it was for her.

And for him.

"Well, I'm a lab tech." She gave a sardonic smile. "See? Not that interesting."

If only she knew how interesting that part of her was to him.

"You sound as if you don't like it."

She shrugged and blew her bangs out of her face before straightening one of his tiles. He raised a brow at that, and she blushed.

"Sorry, I'm a tad OCD according to my friends."

He smiled and shook his head. "It's okay, really."

She huffed out a breath and placed another tile. "I don't hate my job, *exactly*. It's just not that big of a deal." She gave a triumphant smile. "And, I win."

Shade looked into her eyes and groaned. Damn, she was sexy when she looked so confident.

"Indeed you did. Congratulations, Lily." Now for the part that could hurt them both. "How about I buy you a cup of coffee as your winnings?"

Lily looked taken aback, but Shade didn't budge. He needed to know exactly what she knew about this dust. Breaking into her lab and stealing it would do nothing if the dye had already been cast.

"Oh, you don't have to do that. In fact, I don't even know you, so I can't, but thank you."

She gathered the tiles quickly and started to stand up, but Shade touched her wrist. A jolt of electricity ricocheted through his arm and they both gasped. She jumped, knocking a few tiles back on the table. His erection pressed against the zipper of his jeans and he groaned, but he didn't let go. Lily's breathing quickened, and her pupils dilated.

Her strawberry scent wrapped around him like velvet, intoxicating him.

Shade took a deep breath, the strawberry scent increasing, and he released her slowly, one finger at a time. Her chest rose and fell slowly, her breasts straining against her buttoned blouse.

"Sorry, I didn't mean to startle you." He picked up the fallen pieces as she stared at him. "I know you don't know me, but I want to get to know you more." Shade felt the strike against his soul at the truth of the statement that could hurt her. "Please, let me buy you a cup of coffee. It will be in public, and you can leave at any time. What do you say?"

Shade held his breath waiting for her answer.

"Okay," she said tentatively. "I can do that."

Relief spread through him. "I'm glad to hear it. Where would you like to go? I'm not from here, so you tell me."

Lily furrowed her brows. "You're not from here?"

Damn it. Way to show her she was safe with him. "I'm in town on business."

"Oh, I guess we can talk more about that when we get coffee."

"Of course."

"Well, my favorite place is a few miles away, but I walked here. So, let me get my car and we can meet there."

He didn't want her to leave him, and a sweet idea made him harder. "I have a better idea. My bike is just across the park. Let me drive you." He could already feel her soft curves pressed against his back, and he held back a groan.

"Bike?" She gulped.

Shade lifted a side of his mouth in a grin. "I have a Harley Fat Boy, custom made. I always bring it with me when I go on trips." His pride and joy. "I even have an extra helmet in my saddle bags just in case. What do you say?"

Lily swiped her hand through her bangs and bit her lip.

"It'll be an adventure. If you absolutely hate it, I'll make sure I call you a cab to take you home once we finish our coffee."

She looked like she steeled herself while straightening her shoulders. "Okay, I can do that."

Elated, Shade held out his hand to guide her around the table. Her small palm fit perfectly in his calloused hand. A little too perfectly, but Shade couldn't stop and think about that. He released her hand as soon as she made it around the table, careful not to encroach on her space. He could already tell she was a bit skittish; there was no need to scare her away.

She walked by his side, her head down, watching her own steps. Shade bit back a smile as he watched her carefully step over all the cracks.

"Careful not to break your mother's back?" Dear God. Was he trying to drive her away?

She stumbled, tripped, and he moved, catching her. Her soft curves fell against his chest, and he held her a bit tighter before releasing her and setting her on her feet.

"I'm sorry," she mumbled. "I'm such a klutz. I didn't mean to fall on you."

"You're fine, Lily. I shouldn't have made that crack about…well…the cracks."

Lily burst out in a musical laughter, and Shade chuckled.

"I'm a little, well, a lot, OCD. I hate stepping on cracks and grates on top of storm drains. Well, the storm drain part comes from that Stephen King book. I was an idiot and read part of it before bed when I was little. I hate clowns." She shuddered, and Shade held himself back from holding her.

"Clowns freak me out, too." Little did, but the freaks in white paint and red noses? Yeah, those scared the crap out of him. He may be a thousand year old angel, but he was still up on pop culture. Especially because he loved to immerse himself in it.

"Shh!" She grabbed his arm and looked around. "Don't say the 'C' word. They can hear you. Okay, I might have said it before, but don't say it twice. It just makes it worse." She smiled, and he threw his head back and laughed.

"I think I like you, Lily."

She sobered, tilted her head, and looked right into his eyes. "I think I like you too, Shade."

Damn, this was going to hurt when he deceived her. Guilt ate at him.

"Then let's get coffee and talk some more." He smiled, ignoring the pang in his heart.

"I'd like that."

Just then, her cell phone rang, and she frowned. "Sorry, let me get that. It could be one of my friends." She backed away from him and pulled her phone out of her purse.

Lily rocked from foot to foot, her jeans hugging her ass, and Shade swallowed. Damn. His back itched where he kept his wings hidden and he forced them to stay put. This would not be a good time to act like a juvenile and let his wings burst out of his skin just because he got an erection. Talk about embarrassing.

"Glenn," Lily said into her phone, "this is my day off. Why do I need to be in there today?"

Shade eavesdropped and didn't hide it. He needed to know what was going on at her work.

She turned around, sighed, and blew her bangs from her face. "Fine. I'll be here in a bit. I need to go get my car. No, I don't need you to pick me up. I'm fine." She hung up without a goodbye and scowled.

"Is everything all right?"

"No. I'm going to have to take a rain check on coffee. That was my boss. Apparently, there is something important going on at the lab, and I need to head into work. Sorry."

Was it his dust taking her away from him? Damn.

"I understand." He pulled out his phone and smiled. "Why don't you give me your number and I'll call you so you have mine? That way, when you have time, we can get that cup of coffee. Maybe tonight?"

She smiled and rattled off her number. He called her immediately and she silenced it on her phone. "I don't know about tonight. I already have plans with my friends, but maybe tomorrow?"

"Okay. Coffee?"

"Sure. Oh, wait, I have to work all day and then I promised my friends I'd meet them at Dante's Circle to get a drink and help clean up."

"Clean up?"

She shifted uncomfortably, and Shade tilted his head. "There was a storm last night, as you probably know, and it did some damage."

"What kind of damage?"

"The bar was broken up a bit, and it looked like a tornado had gone through."

"Where you there?" His pulse quickened.

"Yeah, but, I'm fine."

Oh, God. Had she been hurt? Shade ran his gaze over her to check for injuries, but he didn't see anything.

"Are you sure?"

"Yes, Shade, I'm fine. Really, but I can't make it for coffee tomorrow either."

He needed to see her sooner rather than later. Yes, for the job, but mostly because he just needed to see her.

"How about I come and meet you at Dante's Circle?"

Her eyes widened slightly. "Okay. Do you know where it is?"

It wasn't that large of a town and couldn't be that hard to find. "I'm sure I can find it. Is nine okay?"

"Nine is perfect. Well…" She bit her lip, and Shade wanted to bite the juicy flesh with her. "I guess I need to be going before Glenn freaks out. I'll see you tomorrow. It was nice to meet you."

"It was nice to meet you, too, Lily."

He took her hand and kissed her knuckles, the warm flesh pressing against his lips sending shivers down his spine and making his wings ache. Along with other things.

He released her hand and smiled. "Until then, Lily."

"Uh…" Lily blinked. "Yes. See you then."

She walked away toward where he assumed her apartment was, stepping on cracks along the way. Apparently, her concentration was on something else. Nice.

"Yes, Lily, until then," he whispered on the wind. Until then.

Dear God, that man was sexier than David Beckham scoring a game-winning goal in the heat and then tearing off his shirt. Yeah. That hot. Lily gripped the steering wheel until her knuckles turned white.

She had a date with Shade. Okay, maybe not a date, more of a get-to-know-you drink at a bar in which they wouldn't be alone, but it still counted. Right? If she really thought about it, their drink would be their second date since they'd just played dominos in the park. But, Lily didn't count that. She wasn't that lucky.

Shade whatever-his-last-name-was was sex on a stick. Lily closed her eyes when she stopped at a red light and tried to compose herself. What was she doing?

Oh, yeah, thinking about that sexy man who'd asked her out on a sort-of-date. He had the body of a swimmer, long, lean, and lickable. Well, she guessed lickable. But, uh, yeah. His darkened skin looked to be natural and not from the sun or a tanning bed. Thank God. She didn't want to date whatever the male equivalent to Snooki was. His midnight black hair hung slightly past his shoulders and swayed in the breeze. Every time she had placed a domino on the board, she'd wanted to reach up and brush her fingers through his hair or down his cheek. He would speak and then give a small smile that had begged her lips for a taste. One look from the man with the ice-blue eyes, and she melted into a puddle.

Oh, his eyes.

They were a crystal blue that seemed to fracture like diamonds from the iris and spiraled into a concentric pattern. She'd never seen anything like them. Simply breathtaking. And, when he stared into her eyes….

A horn honked behind her. She cursed and opened her eyes.

She really needed to get her head out of her behind. She was supposed to be driving for goodness sake. With an apologetic wave to the car behind her, she pressed on the gas and continued on her way to work.

Glenn had called her frantically asking her to come to work and take a look at that blue dust sample he had given her several days before.

Lily pulled into a parking space at work, turned her car off, and closed her eyes. Her body still pulsated from the night at the bar; though why she didn't know. Had the eight of them truly been struck by lightning? Or, was it just a trick of light and a strong wind? Lily didn't know, but so far, other than feeling both rejuvenated and exhausted at the same time, there didn't seem to be any side effects.

She grabbed her purse, locked her car, and ran into the building, careful of the cracks on the ground. If she got through this task early enough, she still had time to clean her living room again before Jamie and Becca showed up for dinner. The girls were coming over to watch a TV show and talk about guys. Well, at least that's what they usually did. Maybe not tonight. Storms had a way of changing things.

When she got to her desk, she locked up her purse, took off her jacket, and pulled on her lab coat. She knew she was alone in the building. A shiver ran up her spine. Though she was an independent woman, being in a large lab alone wasn't her favorite thing in the world. She unlocked her top drawer and pulled out the sample Glenn had given her.

Lily held it up to the light and squinted. What the heck was this stuff? The silver and black flecks interspersed throughout the blue dust seemed to glitter without the assistance of light. Odd.

She shook her bangs from her eyes and shrugged. Well, if she couldn't tell what it was from looking at it, she'd rely on the NMR and data analysis. After all, if people could identify soil and material samples with only their eyes, she'd be out of a job. Lily figured she'd use a dual probe and tune it to carbon and hydrogen. Both of those elements were the most common in materials and would give her a decent basis for what she was trying to identify.

Humming under her breath, she set the sample on her workbench and started to tune the probe. Chemistry wasn't all beakers and explosions. Sometimes she felt like a mechanic with all the wrenches and wires everywhere. After a couple hours, she had the NMR ready for the sample and spun it up to start running the scan.

She sat back in her seat at the computer to watch the scan. It would take a few hours to get everything, but she could at least watch its progress for a bit. Shade's face and his piercing blue eyes flashed across her mind, and she groaned.

Dear Lord, that man was too sexy. Why had he been in the park that morning? Just going for a walk? She had almost left when Jamie texted saying she didn't feel up to playing dominos that morning, but for some odd reason, Lily had stayed a bit longer. Oh, and she was so glad she had.

Damn Glenn for calling her at the most inopportune time. The thought of being on a motorcycle scared her more than flying, but she had really wanted to be behind Shade with her body wrapped around him. She groaned and bit her lip. She shouldn't be having so many dirty thoughts about a man she didn't know; though he did look sort of like the stranger she had envisioned in her dreams…

No, she didn't want to think of that.

Lily blew out a breath and shifted in her seat to take a

look at the sample. For whatever reason, Glenn wanted these results like last week. She looked at the screen and frowned.

What the hell?

There was nothing. No peaks. No shifts. Nothing.

Not a stitch.

No carbon or hydrogen in the entire sample? Almost everything on earth had carbon and hydrogen, if not one, then the other. She couldn't think of any mixture that had *nothing* in it.

What the heck was it?

SHADE DUCKED AS THE TIP OF THE SWORD FLASHED NEAR HIS neck. He lifted his lips in a smile and pivoted, his wings catching a draft and bringing him higher than his opponent. He gripped the hilt tighter and flexed his arm, swinging his blade at his attacker in a firm stroke.

Ambrose changed direction, the blade missing his torso by millimeters. Shade threw back his head and laughed.

"You're getting slow, old friend," he called through the wind.

Ambrose didn't crack a smile, merely tilted his head. "I gave you that one, yet you still missed me. You are not paying attention."

Shade curled his lip. "I'm paying attention just fine. Don't make excuses." He knew Ambrose was right. Shade had too many things on his mind, and he wasn't sparring up to his full potential.

"Is it the woman?"

Shade froze for just a second in the air, the wind blowing through his hair, before he sheathed his sword and lowered himself to the ground behind the house he rented. They were in the back yard and hidden in a copse of trees so the humans couldn't see. He didn't have any neighbors near him so it worked.

"Shade?" Ambrose prompted.

"I'm fine. I met with her in the park and learned a bit more about her." Like the way she blew her bangs from her face when she got nervous. The way her eyes grew bright when she ran high on emotions.

Ambrose landed beside him and quirked a brow, saying nothing. Damn him.

"I don't know what she knows about the dust, but I will find out. I'm going to meet her at her favorite bar, a place called Dante's Circle, tomorrow night. I'll see what I can get from her then." And find out any other personal information he could.

They folded their wings into their backs and walked into the house. Shade went to the kitchen to grab two beers from the fridge. His friend took their swords and placed them in their cases. They drank their beers in silence; Shade's mind was chaotic, his thoughts convoluted with images of Lily's green eyes, soft curves, blue dust, and the war that could come if he couldn't find the answers they desired.

Shade took another drink, the brew sliding down his throat, quenching his thirst. "Did you find anything out about the storm or that odd feeling you had about the origins of the dust?"

Ambrose shook his head then took the last gulp of his beer. "I'm still searching on the lines of your dust issue. Something is not right about this. As for the storm, I don't think it was a normal storm by any means. The electrical currents were too high and not the kind created in a normal weather storm. I believe a bolt of lightning struck, but I'm, as yet, unsure of where it originated, but I will find out, trust me."

Shade nodded. Of course he trusted Ambrose. His white-winged friend was about the only one he could trust.

"Do you want to come with me tomorrow night to Dante's Circle?" Shade asked.

Ambrose nodded. "I think I will. I'd like to meet your Lily."

Shade's pulse increased. "She's not *my* Lily."

His friend lifted a brow. As usual, his friend saw right through him.

No, Lily wasn't his, but that didn't mean he didn't wish it.

STRIKER PACED IN HIS ATRIUM, HIS DRAB BROWN WINGS trailing on the floor. Fury coursed through his veins.

He hadn't liked the intensity of that storm. Something was wrong.

He'd been down to earth, hiding in the clouds and checking on the lab tech's progress with Shade's dust, when that lightning storm had come out of nowhere. The rain had drenched his wings, almost sending him crashing to the ground. He curled his lip at the thought. He'd almost had to walk on the earth like a mere human.

Striker shuddered.

He wasn't a pathetic human; he was an angel. Practically a god. Oh, and once war came, he'd be their ruler, their god. His plans would come to fruition, and he'd own the council. Striker's body shook with anticipation.

That damn storm could prove annoying. There was something in the air that didn't feel right. It was almost a sense of foreboding. The way that lightning had struck that building felt off. The place had brightened for all eyes to see, yet no one seemed to have had noticed for they hadn't come from their homes to see the problem.

Something else was at play.

But what?

Damn it. He didn't have time for the unknown. All these questions were not in his plans. Whatever it was would have to move out of his way because he needed the lab tech to find something and Shade to take the fall. Without that, Shade and his dear friend, Ambrose, would still be in his way.

Something that could not be allowed to happen.

Striker stretched his wings, the dull brown fading

behind the sunlight. He would have to take matters into his own hands and make sure the woman did what she was told. After all, he couldn't trust the humans as far as he could throw them, and due to his strength, that was far. It would still be fun to test that theory. The human woman would do what he wanted, or she'd learn the hard way. Striker smiled. Yes, that would be nice.

CHAPTER 7

Lily eyes drifted shut, and she let her head fall against the headrest. The day seemed to be dragging, never ending. Her body felt like someone had dragged it behind a bus. She'd spent most of the day sitting in her lab trying to figure out just what the heck it was Glenn had given her. None of the readouts made any sense. It was nothing like she'd ever seen, and the computers couldn't figure it out. She'd left it running with another scan overnight to see if she'd made a mistake, but she doubted it. She was OCD enough that things like that didn't happen often, if at all.

A knock on her window brought her out of her thoughts.

"Lily?" Jamie asked through the window. "Are you okay?"

Lily sighed. Was she? She hadn't felt the same since the lightning strike, but she didn't want to say anything else to anyone. What if she were the only one? What would that mean? Frankly, her work issues seemed to be the cause of some of the aches in her body. Her friends didn't need to hear it. It wasn't that they couldn't understand what it was she was experiencing. Well, maybe they could understand, but not really. She'd never could go into details with them about her chemistry theories because their eyes always seemed to glaze over. That seemed true about most people.

She wasn't commenting on her friends' intelligence. No way. Her friends were some of the most brilliant women she'd ever met. Lily just had a different skill set than they did. It wasn't like Jamie would ask her to help her shelve books at the store. Lily might love to read romance novels, just not as much as Jamie, and she couldn't run a business like the quiet woman. They were all so different; it was a wonder that they were all such close friends.

"Lily? What's wrong?" Jamie rapped on the window again, and Lily shook her head.

"Sorry, I'm fine." Lily grabbed her purse, checked her faint makeup in the rearview mirror, and opened the door.

"Are you sure you're okay?" Jamie frowned, brushed her hand against Lily's arm and squeezed.

Sometimes Jamie was more like a sister than a best friend. Lily didn't know what she'd do without her.

"I'm just tired. It was a long day, but I'm better now that I'm here and ready to get a drink."

Jamie gave a small smile. "If you're sure." They walked down the sidewalk toward Dante's Circle's front door. "You look nice tonight. Any special reason?" She smiled knowingly.

"Oh, shut up. You know the reason, but really, do I look okay?"

Jamie pulled her to a halt and looked her over, biting her lip. "Let me see…skinny jeans? Check. Cute flowing top that shows off your curves without making you look skanky? Check. Hot ankle books with that clasp I love? Check. Hair flowing and make up done? Check. Yep, you look incredible. I can't wait to meet this dominos player of yours. Shade." She sighed the last word and fluttered her lashes.

"I knew I never should have told you." Lily fake-scowled.

The night before, Jamie and Becca had come over to watch their weekly airing of *Grey's Anatomy* so they could stare at the sexy blue-eyed doctor, Avery. Forget "McDreamy" and "McSteamy," they wanted "McBlue-Eyes." They hadn't watched most of the show. As soon as Lily had told them of her last-minute replacement dominos partner, Jamie had hit mute and demanded in her quiet way every detail of Mr. Shade.

Lily had described every detail she could. From the way he'd smile and crinkle his eyes to the way the wind touched his hair just right.

And his eyes.

Oh, his eyes.

His crystal-blue eyes put Avery's to shame.

"You're my best friend," Jamie continued. "If you meet Mr. Tall Dark and Handsome, then you have to tell me. It's written in the friend code. I'm sure of it."

Lily wrapped an arm around her friend's shoulder. "Sure, but you'll have to do the same."

Jamie rolled her eyes. "Like that would ever happen. I like lighter hair anyway."

They reached the door and walked in. Lily stopped and looked around the place.

Everything looked like it had before the storm.

What the hell?

How had Dante cleaned everything so fast? They tables and chairs were set where they should have been, the pool table was fixed, and a group of men were racking up the balls. The wood paneling gleamed in the lighting, with not a nick in sight. The pictures were back on the walls set in new frames.

Dante stood behind the bar filling a drink order, but his attention lay solely on Nadie as she frowned at him. Why was she frowning again? Something was going on between the two of them, but Lily didn't know what.

Lily walked toward the two and put her hands on her hips.

"Dante," she called.

He turned his head, grinned, and topped off the beer.

"Good to see you, ladies," he crooned.

Nadie rolled her eyes and took a sip of her club soda.

Jamie went to sit at their normal table, and Lily shook her head and joined her.

"Dante," she started again, "how on earth did you clean up everything so fast?"

He shrugged and brought over their drinks before they even ordered them. "I couldn't sleep. It wasn't that big a deal."

"It was. I mean, look at the place. I don't know how you did it. How did you do it this fast? I thought I was supposed to help." For some reason she felt put out. It wasn't rational.

Dante leaned over and kissed her forehead, and she blushed at the brotherly feel. "I know, sweets. I'll make sure to make a mess later that you can clean up."

"Stop patronizing her," normally calm Nadie ordered.

Dante raised his hands in surrender and backed off. "Let me know if the three of you need anything. Are the rest of your girls coming in?"

Lily shook her head. "No, just the three of us tonight."

He smiled and went back to the bar.

"He's such a jerk sometimes." Nadie scowled.

Lily raised a brow and looked at Jaime, who had an equally confused expression. What the hell? Nadie was the quiet and reserved one. What had Dante done?

"Is there something we should know?" Jamie asked tentatively.

Nadie froze then blushed, a red that flamed out straight to her ears. "No." She coughed. "No, not at all. I just didn't like the way he teased you about your OCD."

Yeah. Sure.

"Okay, if that's all." Lily didn't believe her one bit, but she didn't want to step on any toes. Nadie would let her know what was going on when she felt comfortable. She wouldn't push. It would only further alienate her friend.

"How is everyone feeling?" Lily asked. She'd been feeling slightly off since the lightning strike or whatever the hell that was. Were the others feeling the same?

Nadie shrugged. "Fine, I guess. I don't really know what I'm expecting to feel. I don't feel any different, but I think the fact that I don't feel bad makes me feel like something's wrong, you know?"

Lily nodded. "Exactly."

"It was just a freak storm," Jamie added. "We're fine."

The three looked at each other as unease settled in Lily.

"So, did Lily tell you about the *real* reason she's here tonight?" Jamie asked, a sly smile on her face, breaking the tension.

Lily scowled and threw a pretzel from a bowl that had been on the table when she got there, which the black-haired beauty promptly ducked.

"Hey!" Dante called out. "This isn't the lunchroom cafeteria. No throwing food."

Lily blushed and refrained from throwing one at him. If Becca or Faith had been there, they would have done something, but she didn't have it in her.

"Tell me, Lily." Nadie smiled. "Why are you here?"

"Can't I just come here to talk with my friends?"

"She met a man!" Jamie giggled.

"Ooohhh." Nadie joined in the laugher.

Lily covered her heated face with her hands. It was as if they were twelve. Dear Lord. It wasn't like she never dated. She was old enough to have some experience. Okay, very, *very*, little experience, but geez.

"Shut up, both of you. It's not like that."

"Oh, really?" Nadie raised a brow, a knowing smile on her face. "Then set us straight. How exactly was it?"

Lily let her head fall back and she closed her eyes. What did she expect? These were her best friends, and Shade would be there any minute. She could at least warn them.

"Fine. I met a man named Shade…"

Both women oohed and ahhed at his name, and she threw another pretzel.

"Act like adults!"

"You're the one who just threw food!" Jamie laughed.

"Fine. I won't say anything else."

Nadie's eyes widened, and she failed at hiding her smile. "I'll be good. I promise. Tell me more about Shade."

"I met him in the park. He's just a guy who played dominos with me."

"He was going to take our Lily on a motorcycle ride," Jamie added.

"Our Lily on a motorcycle? He must be amazing," Nadie said

Lily let a sigh slip. "Oh, he was, no *is*. I don't know. I mean, I don't know him. He offered to take me for coffee, but then I got called into work. Now he's coming here soon so everything worked out I guess."

"He's coming here?" Nadie asked.

"Yep, any minute now."

"Hence the cute clothes." Nadie nodded.

"Are you saying I look like crap most days?"

"No, it's just that you look all datey."

"Datey is not a word," Jamie, their loving bookstore owner, corrected.

Nadie rolled her eyes, very reminiscent of the kindergarten students she taught. "I know that, I was just in the mood to make one up. You do look nice, Lily."

"Thank you, Nadie." She just hoped Shade thought so too. He was so handsome she felt sort of unworthy. A stupid thing to think of since she was an independent, modern woman. Still…

Nadie scrunched her brows. "Wait, why did you have to go into work? I thought it was your day off."

Anger rose through her at the thought. "Yes, but Glenn called me in to work on this special project of his."

"What an ass," Nadie said, and blushed. The woman never cursed.

"Yeah, but there's nothing I can do about it. He's my boss, and I need the job."

"So, what was so special about this project?"

She shrugged. "I don't know. It's just this odd sample that's not showing up clearly on any of the scans I've run. I'm doing them again to make sure I didn't make a mistake."

Jamie sat forward. "You don't make mistakes like that, Lily. Maybe it was something else." Her eyes brightened with anticipation.

"This isn't one of your mystery novels, Jamie."

She waved a hand around. "It could be. Shade can be your mystery man that will help you solve the case." She sat back and sighed. "Isn't it romantic?"

"You really need to get your head out of your books." Lily smiled at the thought of being side-by-side with Shade as they solved the case of the mysterious blue dust. Then when they figured out what it was, they could celebrate…

Images of his tanned skin brushing against hers, his hands tangling in her hair as he crushed his mouth to hers, the way he would thrust into her…

Lily choked on her soda, and Jamie stood to slap her on the back.

"Sexy thoughts?" Nadie asked.

"Shut up," Lily rasped out.

"I can't wait to meet this Shade of yours," Jamie said.

"He's not *my* Shade."

"Not yet, anyway." Nadie smiled.

As nice as it would be, Lily didn't want Shade to be hers. He was just a hot guy she'd met at a park. They hadn't even been on a real date. Tonight wouldn't count. He was meeting her with her friends in a public place. Not quite the ideal romantic situation. She was getting ahead of herself anyway. Shade hadn't really shown any interest. Heated glances aside, she didn't know anything about him. Why would he want her? He could have any woman he wanted, and she was just plain, practically virginal Lily.

Tonight would just be a meeting of minds where she could talk to him. That was it. Nothing would come of it. She probably wouldn't even see him again.

Yep. That's what would happen. She probably wouldn't ever see him again; him and his piercing blue eyes and sexy-as-hell motorcycle. Nope. Wouldn't happen.

A pang shot through her heart. She was human enough to admit that she wanted it to happen, but want did not equal getting, especially to a woman like her. She was just average. Average body, hair, personality. Average everything. She'd been through the whole 'loving a man' thing before only to find out he was a loser. She didn't want to go through that again.

Lily checked her cell phone for the fifth time. Ten more minutes. She could wait that long and then he'd leave soon after, most likely. If he even showed.

That would be his choice. She'd be fine. See? She was acting like a calm, rational adult.

Right?

God, this self-pity made her feel like crap.

"Let me get this straight." Ambrose's deep voice penetrated the silence of the car. "I'm to be your wingman?" He lifted a blonde brow, and Shade held back a chuckle.

They were on their way to Dante's Circle to meet Lily and try to see if they could get information out of her.

Shade tried not to smile.

Lily.

He couldn't lie to himself. He also just wanted to see her again. The strawberry scent of her made him want to lick every inch of her to see if she tasted the same. Yes, he'd find out what he needed for the council, but he also wanted to get to know her.

Hell. He *really* didn't want to do this to her. Why did the only woman that had caught his eye in decades also have to be the one who could be his people's downfall?

Fate sucked ass sometimes.

Okay, all the time.

"Shade? If you are as lost inside your head with the girl as you are now, it's no wonder you haven't found out anything."

He shook his head and gave a quick glare to Ambrose before switching lanes. It might be true that Lily occupied his thoughts more than she should, but that didn't mean he wasn't good at his job. He was a warrior, meaning he protected his brethren from all forces. Even if he didn't have to use a sword to get his way, he still had a job to do. It grated on him that his friend and mentor would think so lowly of him.

"We're almost there," he growled.

"I trust you, Shade. It's just that I don't trust this situation. It's keeping me on edge. I know that you'll find out what we need to know and retrieve everything. Our secrets are safe as long as we figure out what's going on."

Shade nodded, his anger receding at his mentor's words. He pulled up to the bar and parked. The wind blew leaves across his windshield, but it was a far cry from the weather of a few nights ago, and it wasn't raining.

They got out of the car and walked along the sidewalk toward the entrance. Ambrose looked around, ever the watchful warrior, as Shade steeled himself for what was to come. Keeping the supernatural secret was more important than just one woman and one angel. He needed to remember that, and to swallow any emotion that might want to say otherwise. He'd do anything he could to get the information.

The mission had to be a success.

They entered the bar, and Shade looked around. It seemed welcoming and not dingy, but something seemed a bit off. Something…what was that? An inexplicable energy rode on the air. A metallic taste settled on his tongue, and the hairs on his arms stood.

"Ambrose?"

"I feel it, too. Whatever happened here was recent, but isn't here now."

Shade nodded. He trusted Ambrose's statement.

Shade inhaled, and a soft strawberry scent tickled his nose.

Lily.

He smiled even though a heavy weight settled in his stomach.

Here it goes.

He walked toward the back table where Lily sat with a petite blonde woman and a dark-haired woman; all three seemed to radiate with an undercurrent of an unknown energy. The energy crackled and danced along his skin like static electricity.

Odd.

Even though he thought both women were attractive, they didn't hold a candle to his Lily.

No.

Just Lily. There was no *his* about it.

She turned, and her bright green eyes lit up. "Shade. You

made it."

Shade swallowed hard then gave his best playboy grin. "Of course I'm here. I said I would be. It's good to see you." He walked toward her and held out his hand.

She smiled and placed her small hand in his. He could feel her pulse racing, and he was glad he wasn't the only one feeling their connection.

"Oh." She bit her lip. He released her hand, and she brushed her bangs out of her face. He loved that nervous gesture.

"This is my friend Ambrose." He gestured to his friend, but Ambrose's attention seemed to be on the dark-haired woman. He had a curious expression on his face.

Shade elbowed him, and Ambrose looked up abruptly then shook his head.

"Hello, ladies."

"Nice to meet you," Lily said. "These are my friends, Jamie and Nadie. Take a seat."

Shade nodded at the two women and took a seat next to Lily, her tantalizing scent washing over him as he scooted closer. Ambrose took a seat next the petite blonde woman and gave his normal neutral expression.

"So, this is Dante's Circle." Lily smiled and looked nervous, and Shade wanted to kiss her to make her feel better.

So not the time. Maybe later.

"I like it," Shade answered honestly. It was a really nice looking place. The dark wood features seemed to grab the patrons and make them want to ask for a drink. It was as if he was at home hanging out with his friends and just wanted to feel good. Whoever owned the place must have had that in mind; or maybe they were just really lucky.

Lily beamed, and Shade tamped down the nervous energy in his gut about lying to her. He couldn't think about that now.

"Tell us about yourself, Shade," Jaime said, her deep brown eyes inquisitive.

Ah, Lily's champion. He liked this one already.

The other woman, Nadie, leaned forward and gripped the sides of her glass in a nervous motion, but seemed interested in what Shade had to say. He liked her, as well. They cared for Lily.

"I'm in town for business and met Lily in the park, but I'm sure you already know that." Shade lifted his lip in a small smile. He wasn't lying; he just wasn't going to tell them *exactly* why he was there.

"So, you're leaving soon?" Nadie looked a bit sad at the prospect and shot Lily a glance.

"I'm not sure yet, but I won't leave for a while. I know that much."

Lily smiled, and Shade followed the long curve of her neck with his gaze. What would her skin taste like if he licked and nibbled right where her neck met her shoulder? Would she shudder in his arms and whisper his name?

Shade shifted in his seat as his erection dug into his zipper, and his wings threatened to pop out of his back. He needed to focus on his assignment and not the sexy creature in front of him.

"I'm glad you'll be around for a bit longer," Lily said and blushed. "I mean, you get to see the city and all."

Jamie coughed and took a sip of her drink.

God, Lily was cute.

"I'm quite boring, actually," Shade continued. The more he talked about himself, the easier it would be for Lily to open up about her own likes and dislikes. And work. He couldn't forget the real reason he was here. "I play dominos in the park." Shade grinned, and Lily blushed. "I also ride my motorcycle when I can." *Or I fly.* "I work, I read, and I design rock sculptures."

The women stared at him as if he had a second head, or he had sprouted wings. He looked over his shoulder. Nope. Still hidden.

"What did I say?" Shade asked.

"What do you design?" Lily asked.

"Oh, well, I cut rock and build different waterfall sculptures for people." Shade shrugged. He hadn't meant to let that last piece slip, but he couldn't seem to keep much from Lily. Not a good thing. "It's just a hobby. I don't get to do it as much as I like. I like working with my hands."

Lily's pupils dilated, and Shade held back a groan.

He wanted her. Now.

"What can I get you two to drink?"

A deep voice pulled Shade way from Lily's green eyes, and Shade started.

Holy. Shit.

The tattooed man raised a brow, and Shade blinked. "Uh, anything you have on tap is good with me."

"Me, as well," Ambrose added, a scowl on his face.

"Shade, this is Dante," Lily said, unaware of the tension. "He owns the bar and is our friend."

Friend?

His Lily was friends with a fucking dragon?

Interesting.

"Dante, this is Shade and Ambrose," Lily continued. "When you get a minute, you can join us if you want."

Nadie scowled and Shade just sat there. Her friends were more than they thought, weren't they? At least the bartender.

What an interesting night.

"I'll be sure to stop by," Dante answered. "Let me get your drinks, boys."

Boys? How old was this dragon if he thought Shade was a boy? What did he have to do with Lily?

Dante squinted and glared at the two men before he stalked off to get their drinks.

"What was that about?" Jamie asked. "He's usually in a good mood. It must be because of what happened to the bar." She quickly shut her mouth and widened her eyes.

"What happened?" Ambrose asked.

Lily coughed and took a drink. "The place was damaged a bit in the storm a couple of nights ago, but everything is fine." She stressed the last word, and Shade felt like he and Ambrose were missing something.

"Were you all here?" Ambrose asked.

Lily looked at him and paled a bit. "Um, yes."

"I'm glad you're okay. I mean, you are okay, right?"

"Of course. Perfectly healthy. It was just scary there for a moment."

Shade couldn't help it. He placed his hand on hers on the table, turned it over, and rubbed small circles in her palm. Her pulse picked up, and her lips parted.

"I'm glad to hear it."

Her soft skin felt smooth against his calloused fingers. He wanted to see if she were smooth everywhere.

"Lily, what do you do for a living?" Ambrose's voice broke Shade from his thoughts.

Dammit. He needed to focus. It was just so hard with the woman beside him.

Speaking of hard…

No. Dammit.

What kind of warrior angel was he?

Not a good one, apparently.

"Oh, I'm just a lab tech," Lily answered, her face flushing as she pulled her hand away to grip her drink.

Shade immediately felt the loss of contact.

"Working on anything interesting?"

God. Subtle much?

Lily furrowed her brows. "Actually, we just got a new sample. I'm not allowed to talk about it other than it's taking up a lot of my time."

Shade's pulse raced.

Shit. She'd already started the analysis.

"Can you tell what it is?"

She shook her head. "Not yet, but I'll find out."

It was as he feared. She couldn't be allowed to know any

more. He and Ambrose would have to break in and take the sample and her files before she found out any more. If she found out anything else...

He didn't want to think about it.

His job as a warrior angel was not for the weak-hearted.

He might just be weak-hearted for the green-eyed girl in front of him.

"I'm sure you will," Shade finally responded, though he didn't sound too sure.

"Here's your drinks." Dante set the two beers in front of Shade and Ambrose before walking around the circular table to sit next to Nadie. She frowned and stirred her drink again.

Whatever was going on between the two of them wasn't his business. The thought of a dragon liking the innocent woman in front of him made Shade want to laugh, though he didn't. One did not laugh at a dragon and walk away, not even a millennia-old angel.

Shade took a sip of the hoppy brew and smiled. Nice. The dragon had good taste.

"Good?" Lily asked.

"Very. Your friend has good taste."

She smiled, and he gave into temptation and brushed a lock of hair behind her ear. She shivered, and he smiled. So responsive.

Dammit. His job was nearing its end in terms of her part. He'd have to break into her workplace soon, and he would never be able to see her again.

He'd have to talk to Ambrose. His mentor would have an

idea of what to do. No matter what, Shade couldn't be done with Lily. He needed a taste of her.

"When are you free again?" Shade asked.

Ambrose scowled in his direction. Shade didn't care. He needed to see this woman again. Shade hadn't done anything for himself in so long; he needed this.

"Um, I don't know." She bit her lip, and Shade wanted to taste the juicy flesh.

"How about tomorrow?"

"I think I can do that."

He could feel the gazes of the four people at their table, but Shade ignored them. Yes, it was awkward asking a woman out with an audience such as theirs, but he'd do it again in a heartbeat.

"How does dinner sound?"

"Great."

"I can pick you up at six if you'd like."

"On your motorcycle?" she asked, eagerness in her tone.

He bit back a groan at the thought of her legs wrapped around his bike and then him.

"That can be arranged."

"Okay, that sounds nice." She smiled shyly, and he smiled back.

He took a sip of his beer, the rest of their party doing the same.

He had a date with a pretty green-eyed woman.

He only had to make sure they didn't take down the entire supernatural race in the process.

Crap.

CHAPTER 9

S hade groaned as he lifted another rock into position, the heavy weight settling against the other boulder snuggly. He was frustrated beyond all reality.

He had a date that night with Lily, but the following night he'd have to betray her and never see her again.

That was what he and Ambrose had decided.

The lab was closed for the day so no testing and results would be taken. It gave him the reprieve he so desperately needed. The thought of what he was about to do made him sick to his stomach.

If things went well, he'd sleep with a beautiful woman and then break her heart. As much as he wanted to sleep with her, he didn't think he could. Not without finding a way to make it last longer...

That didn't look like an option though.

Who was this angel?

Not him, surely.

He wasn't acting like himself. It was as if an invisible cord pulled him toward Lily, making him do things he didn't normally do. Maybe it was fate.

He cursed. Fate? Was he really resorting to that as an excuse for his poor behavior?

A bare-chested Shade lifted another rock, his muscles bulging. It wasn't too heavy for an angel like him, but it was still awkward lifting it. He set it down and maneuvered the stone into position. When he was done, the backyard would have a decent rock sculpture and waterfall. He'd start chiseling a bit later. Now, he just wanted to use up his pent-up energy.

Shade pulled back and stretched his wings. They didn't have any neighbors and he needed to feel the wind against his feathers. He bent then lifted himself to the sky, his body finding a drift in the air. He closed his eyes, his body going beneath his shield so the world couldn't see him. He loved the feel of weightlessness as he arched his body around a cloud to avoid getting wet. His hair whipped around him. He should have tied it back because it would be a bitch to untangle when he got back to get ready for his date.

He looked at his blue-tipped wings and sighed; at least he wasn't trailing dust this time. It only happened in times of great stress or emotion. Despite all that was going on, he had to keep his emotions in check.

Ambrose was out trying to determine if there were any connections between the council and their assignment. Something just didn't sit right with either of them. How did the human male, Glenn, get his dust in the first place? Shade couldn't believe that he'd just stumbled upon it. To the untrained eye, an angel's dust might look benign, even with the special colors and flecks, but someone had seen it and collected it, and the council had found out about it. Shade spread his wings and shot up vertically, and then he tucked his wings close to his body and dove, gravity pulling him down like a lead weight. He arched and twisted, his body breaking through the air like a bird in flight, and then he spread his wings and landed on his feet.

Adrenaline coursed through his system as his body acclimated to being back on the ground.

The image of green eyes flittered through his brain, and he cursed.

What the hell was going on? Why was he so attracted to her? There was this strange energy around her and her friends at the bar. Something he couldn't name, but it felt important to him. They were human, well, as human as anyone could be. Still...

Green eyes faded to hazel and Shade froze.

Cora.

His fiancée.

Well, fiancée of the past.

The Angelic Wars had taken her with them. She wasn't around anymore to yell at him for not paying attention to his assignment.

She was dead.

He hadn't truly thought about her in ages. The Angelic Wars had ended over eight-hundred years ago, and she'd been gone just as long. Why was he thinking of her now? Because of Lily?

She didn't have Lily's smile. No, Lily was warm while Cora had been cool; but then Cora had been a warrior like him. She could fight better than anyone he'd known except for Ambrose and himself. She had been fierce and intelligent with harsh curves. Not like Lily or his own sister, Ilianya.

Shade sighed and held his head in his hands. Ilianya had been a soft angel, the softest. His sister had married a cool and collected angel: his best friend, Ambrose. She and Ambrose had had two children, a son named Nathan, and a daughter, Laura. Ilianya had been pregnant with their third when the Angelic Wars had taken her and the children. No one had been safe. The battles hadn't been fought on some distant plane or battlefield. No, they'd happened at their front doors and in their homes. That's why the cost had been so high. They'd not only lost warriors, but their families, as well.

Shade held back a sob. He hadn't cried for them in centuries. There wasn't any point. Tears wouldn't bring Cora back, wouldn't bring the sound of children laughing, or his sister singing while she danced in air. It wouldn't bring any of that back.

Shade closed his eyes and fought back the memories.

"Shade, you'll have to do better than that to catch me." Cora gave a cool smile then winked before jumping off the ledge, the wind catching her gray wings.

Shade laughed and jumped behind her, the cool breeze

catching him on a draft. "I do not need to catch you, Cora. You will come to me eventually."

She twisted in the air then landed on a ledge. "Cocky."

Shade landed beside her and lifted a brow. "Just stating the facts." He took a deep breath and stepped toward her, but he didn't touch her. "I don't want you to be fighting in this next battle."

She threw up her hands cursing under her breath. "Every time, Shade. Every time. It's so frustrating! I'm a warrior angel. I may be forty years younger than you, but I'm way past the age of adulthood. I'm capable of doing this. Are you doubting me?"

Shade pinched the bridge of his nose. "I know you can do this, Cora. I just have a bad feeling about this particular battle. Can't you stay behind with Ilianya? Just this once?"

Cora stood toe-to-toe with him, an icy glint in her eyes. "I will do what I have to, to protect our people. Don't stand in my way, Shade. You may love me, but that doesn't give you the right to control me."

He sighed and lowered his head. "Just be careful."

"I always am."

Shade pulled himself from his memoires. It would do no good to dwell on them. Cora was long gone. His job now was to make sure he kept Lily ignorant of the truth about him and his mission. He could fall for her; he knew it. He couldn't allow that to happen because those he loved always died. Not to mention he was an angel and she was a human. He'd live for eons and she'd die tomorrow or in a matter of decades. He didn't want to watch her grow old while he stayed young. It wasn't fair to either of them. Lily was already in danger. He didn't need to add anything else to the pile.

THE RAIN POURED DOWN OUTSIDE HER APARTMENT, AND LILY shuddered. Thank God she and Jamie decided to stay in and play dominos. She set down a double-three piece and smiled. She was almost out of pieces and Jamie still had a few more, though Lily had an odd amount of pieces and that was frustrating because even numbers were better. She let the thought of the other numbers on the board calm her. Yes, she was OCD, but she dealt with it in her own way.

Nausea rolled through her, and she flexed her fingers and closed her eyes. It had been like this since the lightning strike. They should have gone to the hospital right away. For some reason, they had all decided that they would be fine. It had been as if some invisible force had held them back. Even now, when she thought about going to see a doctor, something in the back of her mind urged her not to go.

Whatever it was, it made her nervous, but not as much as the thought of her date that night with Shade, a man she barely knew. Who was this woman? Certainty not Lily Banner, the OCD lab tech who had only had one prior relationship—a relationship that had gone nowhere because she had been too blind to see what was in front of her. Lily was a good girl. Yet every time she saw Shade, she wanted to be naughty. Real naughty.

Yes, it was just a date with Shade. That's all he said anyway. Then she remembered the molten looks and the tingling touches, and she wanted to melt on the spot. She had a feeling she wouldn't be sweet Lily after she went out with Shade. No, she'd be wanton Lily. She was okay with that.

Well, mostly.

She really, really wanted Shade. He was the man of her dreams, literally. She'd seen her blue-eyed man before. That night after the lightning had struck, she'd seen a face in her dreams. Shade's face. It hadn't been too clear, but now that she thought about it, she knew it had been him.

Was it fate's way of saying she should take a chance with him?

She smiled. No, she couldn't think that way. It was just a coincidence. Shade was just a blue-eyed, dark-haired stranger. There were tons of them in the world. Shade wasn't anything special.

Now she was just lying to herself.

There was something odd about this stranger. She couldn't put her finger on it. It was as if a weird energy surrounded him; which made it even odder since she normally didn't notice that type of thing. Maybe it was just the fact that he was ultra-sexy and those were hunky vibes or something.

"Lily? It's your turn." Jamie waved her hand in front of Lily's face, and Lily blinked.

"Oh, sorry. I was distracted." She looked down at her pile

and carefully placed her pieces so the edges matched perfectly.

"Really?" Her friend grinned, and Lily blushed. "Are you thinking about Shade?"

Lily sighed and closed her eyes. "Yes, you know it. God, what am I doing? I don't even know this man, and I'm going on a date with him."

Jamie picked another piece from the boneyard and then played it. "You know him enough, Lily. That's what dating is for; to get to know people. Unless you start dating your best guy friend, you're pretty much going to meet a stranger."

"That doesn't alarm you in any way?" She set down another piece and straightened it.

"Of course it does. What was the last time you've seen me on date?"

"True."

Jamie stuck out her tongue. "Jerk. You're a nun just like me."

"Until recently."

"So, Lily, what did you think about drinks last night? You at least had a little bit of fun, didn't you?"

Lily smiled and bit her lip. "It was so nerve-wracking. What was I thinking having him come to my favorite place and meet my friends? Isn't that supposed to be date five or something?"

Her friend shrugged and ran a hand through her bangs. "I'm not sure. You were going to go out to coffee with him until Glenn called, so it wasn't as if you had planned it that way. Plus, we're very protective of you, and you didn't invite Faith. You saved Shade with that one."

They laughed, and Lily shook her head. "You're bad. Completely correct, but bad."

"I try."

"Last night was fun. I mean you got to meet Shade and his friend Ambrose. What did you think of him anyway?"

Jamie blushed. *Interesting.* "He was okay."

"Really? Just okay?"

"Okay, he was hot. There. I said it."

Lily laughed. "He was hot, though the white-blonde hair isn't my thing."

"I know, you like the dark and mysterious type, hence Shade, but I think I like blonds. Or, in Ambrose's case, the really blond. Not that it matters."

"Why?"

"Uh, have you looked at me? I'm about the plainest person you've ever seen. Ambrose didn't even notice me unless he glared at me."

"Okay, you're not plain. Shut up. When did this happen?"

"If you had bothered to take your eyes of Shade for a moment, you would have noticed, but it's okay. Really."

Damn. Talk about being a bad friend. "I'm sorry, Jamie."

She waved her hand in front of her face. "It's fine. I was probably imagining it anyway."

"Well, I'm sorry anyway."

"At least I wasn't in Nadie's shoes last night?"

"What do you mean? How much did I miss last night?"

Jamie smiled and put a piece down. "I'm glad to see you

were so focused. Haven't you noticed Nadie has been acting odd whenever she's in the bar?"

Lily thought about it. "You know, she has been acting odd; like she has a shorter temper or something."

"Could it be because of what happened?"

Lily shook her head. "No, it started before that. Oh, and that reminds me, what was with Dante last night?"

"I know! He was acting so territorial and growly toward Ambrose and Shade. I was surprised he didn't mark his territory or something."

"Eww. Totally not okay. Maybe it's something along those lines though. I think it's because Shade and Ambrose are the first men any of us have brought around. Maybe he was just jealous or something."

"Like he wants you?"

Lily laughed. "Oh, no. I meant like he was the only guy of our group, you know."

"Ah, and then these two sexy men come waltzing into his life. I could see that being it."

"Whatever it was, I just hope he doesn't get his feelings hurt."

"Lily, Dante is a big boy; he'll be okay."

"If you're sure." A sharp pain, a sort of energy, surged through her, and settled in her stomach. She groaned and her body jerked. It felt as if someone had pushed her into an electric fence.

"Lily? Are you okay?"

She opened her mouth to speak, and a piercing pain

stabbed her temple. She shook her head and stood on wobbly legs.

"Lily, what's the matter?"

Ignoring her friend's worried tone, she stumbled to the bathroom, her body breaking out in a cold sweat.

She made it to the bathroom, locked the door behind her, and gripped the rim of pedestal sink, her vision graying.

Oh, God, what was going on? She didn't need to throw up, but just as her body felt as though it had been drained of energy, that vibrating current surged through her again. She glanced up, and her reflection in the mirror made her gasp. Her normally pale skin appeared even more stark, but now it had also been tinged with a green hue. However, that wasn't what made her want to scream.

Her skin rippled like the sea at the beginning of a storm. Little tinges of static energy popped and lit up the room like tiny fireworks.

She closed her eyes and took a deep breath, trying to calm down, but her body shivered and broke out into a cold sweat. Minutes later, her body calmed, and a banging sound make her open her eyes.

"Lily! Open the door!" Jamie yelled.

Lily took a look at her reflection, and she appeared normal, just a bit sweaty. With shaky hands, she opened the door to a wide-eyed Jamie.

"What's going on? Were you sick?" She grabbed Lily's hand and led her to the toilet. Lily sat on the lid and lay back against the cool porcelain.

"I think so. I just felt a little off. I'm feeling better now."

"You scared me when you locked the door. Don't do that again." Jamie placed a cool wet washcloth on her forehead, and Lily smiled.

"Yes, Mom."

"Damn straight. Really, Lily, what's wrong?"

Lily sighed and rubbed her temples. "I don't know. This is the first time that's happened. I have been feeling a bit more tired lately. Since…you know."

Jamie nodded, her eyes full of a quiet understanding. "Well, I haven't had any of what you've been having, hon."

"You do look a bit more tired this morning."

"Gee, thanks."

"You know what I mean."

"I do, and yes, I'm a bit tired today, but nothing like what you have."

"It's just a bit troubling."

"I know, hon, but we'll figure it out. We have to."

Something was going on, and Lily was nervous as hell to figure out what. If what had just happened was only the beginning, she was in trouble.

CHAPTER 10

"What about this one?" Becca held up a red scooped-neck dress that Lily hadn't worn in years.

"Not this time," Lily answered. "He's picking me up on his bike; I can't wear a dress." Her body warmed at the thought of Shade on his Harley, and she smiled.

"Oh, I remembered, but I thought you could have fun with it anyway." Becca winked and put the dress back in the closet.

Becca had come over a few hours after Lily had started feeling better from her episode in the bathroom to help her and Jamie get ready for Lily's date. She and Jamie had decided not to mention what had happened to Becca for the time being since it would just worry their friend.

Lily would have to sit down with everyone at some point and tell them what was going on. As much as she'd like to, she couldn't bury her head in the sand anymore, though the idea seemed more appealing with each passing moment.

"Okay, then," Becca continued, "are we going for slutty or cute?"

Jamie laughed and set down a sliver-glitter top and a white jean jacket on the bed in front of Lily.

"How about sexy cute?" Lily asked.

Oh, God. Why had she said yes to Shade? Her palms were sweating as if it was her first ever date. She'd been engaged for God's sake.

None of her experiences could prepare her for Shade.

Lily drifted to the bathroom and changed into the clothes Jamie had picked out. The top and jacket set went perfectly with skinny jeans and silver boots. She'd blown out her hair and then clipped it on the base of her neck so she could wear a helmet and still look okay. Well, at least she hoped. Maybe Shade wouldn't care about helmet hair.

At least her boobs looked good in this top. That was something.

She walked back to her bedroom and did a slow twirl. "So, what do you think?"

"You look great, hon," Jamie said.

Becca wrapped an arm around Jamie's shoulder and dried an imaginary tear from the corner of her eye. "They grow up so fast, don't they?"

They all laughed, and Lily walked to her dresser to put in some small silver hoops.

There. She was ready. Well, as ready as she could get. She picked her up small purse and put everything in it.

She'd either snap it under her jacket or put it in a side bag if Shade had one. She looked around her room and straightened the already smoothed out cream bedspread and flicked off an imaginary fuzz ball.

"Your house is as immaculate as always, Lily. Stop worrying," Jamie said.

"Yep. It's perfect, which is good because since Shade is just in town for a bit, he may not have a place to take you afterward." Becca wiggled her eyebrows, and Lily blushed.

A soft pang entered her heart at the thought that Shade wouldn't be here for long. She had to remember that. He wasn't here to stay. He'd be gone soon, and Lily would be alone with her ODC and her thoughts.

"Lily, stop that." Jamie smiled.

"I know. I just need to think about tonight and not the future. It's just a date and I need to have fun."

"That's the spirit," Becca said. "Okay, we need to go before he gets here. Keep your cellphone on and be careful. Don't do anything I wouldn't do, and if you do, make sure you take pictures." She winked and gave her a hug, Jamie following soon after.

Her friends left, and Lily was alone in her home, nervous as all hell. A moment later, a knock at the door startled her, and her pulse quickened.

He was here.

Okay, you can do it. Just don't throw up.

Lily laughed. That was a great thing to think before a date. She opened a door with a smile on her face then froze in her tracks.

He was even more handsome now. How on earth was that possible?

His midnight black hair hung loose, framing his face. He wore a black button-down shirt tucked into jeans with the sleeves rolled up so she could see his forearms. Damn, she wanted to lick them. Just a little taste.

Who knew forearms were sexy?

His dark jeans encased thick thighs and make her think of what else could be thick…

She raised her head and blushed.

Oh. God.

"Hi." Shade smiled and tilted his head.

"Hi," she said on a quiet exhale.

"You look beautiful, Lily." He tucked a stray hair behind her ear, and she shivered.

"You do, too." She blushed again. Soon she'd be Crayola red. "I mean you look handsome."

He traced her jaw with a calloused finger. "Thank you. Are you ready to go?"

She swallowed hard. "Uh-huh."

Okay, she really had to remember the English language. This was getting embarrassing.

"Okay, then." He trailed his hand down her arm and wrapped his hand around hers. His warm skin felt like heaven against hers.

She shook her head, clearing her thoughts. How was she supposed to get through a whole date if she couldn't even formulate enough of a conversation to get out of the door?

With a nod, she gripped his hand tighter and closed the door behind her. He led her to his bike, and she smiled.

"I love it, Shade."

He gave a huge grin. "Thanks. This is my baby. No matter where I am, I try and take her with me." He rubbed the leather seat, and an irrational urge to knock the bike down went through her.

She would *not* be jealous of a motorcycle. Would not.

"So, here is your helmet." He placed it on her head and fixed the strap beneath her chin, his fingers grazing her skin. "I have some night glasses for you." He placed yellow-lensed glasses on her face and he smiled. "I know they aren't too fashionable, but they will keep the wind out of your eyes and help with glare."

"That makes sense, thanks. I've never been on a bike before."

"I'll show you, baby." *He called me baby!* "I'm going to get on first and stand the bike up straight. When I say so, I want you to put your left hand on my left shoulder, and your left foot on the peg." He pointed down to show her where the peg was located. "And then, throw your right leg over the seat.. If you need to move around, just do it is small movements, okay? My feet are planted, so we won't fall."

He got on the bike. She watched his thighs bunch as he righted the bike. She licked her lips. This was going to be a long night.

"Ready, Lily?"

She followed his instructions and got on behind him.

His heated body lay flush against her, and she held back a groan.

"Wrap your arms around my waist," Shade said.

She did so, and she clasped her hands together so they wouldn't roam the hard planes of his chest.

"Okay, hold on and lean with me in the turns. I'm going to go slow, but we'll be okay. Just do what I do, and you'll be fine." He patted her hand then started the bike.

The vibrations rumbled right to her core and she gasped. Dear God. Was this why people loved riding? She might have to get one of her own.

He pulled out onto the street, and Lily held tighter. It was so invigorating. The wind lashed against her face, and she felt like she was flying. She wasn't scared like she normally would be. Maybe it was because she was with Shade. He revved the engine, the vibrations running through her body, and she almost squealed in delight. This was so much fun! The wind grew colder and she buried closer to the heat radiating off Shade's body. Oh, boy, he was hot; in more ways than one.

They drove on and she leaned with him into a turn, his hard body pressed against hers. Apparently, riding a motorcycle was a form of foreplay. Who knew?

They finally pulled up to a Korean restaurant she loved. How did he know?

He turned off the bike, planted his feet, and turned toward her. "You okay back there?"

"I'm great." Really. She had never felt better.

"Okay, so get off like you got on, and you should be fine."
She did, and took off her helmet and shook out her hair.

Helmet hair. Terrific.

She re-clipped it and took off her glasses to give to Shade. He locked up the equipment and held her hand.

"I didn't know exactly what you liked, but this place sounded good."

"Oh, this is one of my favorite places. Their bulgogi is perfect."

"Then I'm glad I chose it."

They walked directly to a table since it was first come-first serve seating. Shade pulled out her chair for her, and she fell just a little bit more for him. Her heart sped a bit, and her palms grew damp. Dangerous.

"I'm glad you came, Lily." Shade grinned and rubbed small circles in her wrist.

His decadent chocolate scent wrapped around her and she shuddered. She didn't know why she could pinpoint his exact scent, but she loved it. Tendrils of pleasure crawled up her arms and her body. She did her best not to jump over the table and molest him. It was hard, but she did it.

"I'm glad I did, too."

"What do you usually get here?"

"Oh, anything is good. I like the dak bulgogi. It's like a soup version of their barbecue beef."

"What if I get the bulgogi and some dumplings and we share?"

"Perfect."

The waiter came with water and took their orders.

"Did you have fun last night?" she asked. Oh, God, why did she ask that? What if he hated it and this was just a pity date? She bit her lip and tried not to look like she was on the verge of a panic attack.

This was why she didn't date. Well, that and the fact nobody asked her other than her lab partner, Thad.

Shade took a sip of his water. "Yes. I like your friends."

She warmed. "I'm glad. They liked you, too."

They talked about her work, her hobbies, touched a bit on her childhood, and ate. Their conversation strayed away from him, but Lily didn't care. The food was good, and her companion was caring and sexy. She could learn more about him later.

When the check came, he paid, held out his hand, and she followed him outside. "What would you like to do now, Lily?" he asked, his voice hoarse and low, sending shivers down her spine.

She gulped. "Well, there is a park near my house. Do you want to go for a walk?"

He gave a nod and traced her jaw with his finger. The calloused tip scraped against skin, sending shivers down her spine. "As long as I get to spend more time with you, I'm happy."

When he said things like that, it was hard for her to remember that he would be leaving.

They rode back to her place, and he held her hand as they walked toward the park.

"I'm glad I came out tonight, Shade." Her heart rate sped

up and she prayed her hands weren't too sweaty from nervousness.

He stopped and turned toward her then framed the side of her face in one large warm hand. His pupils widened, and his lips parted. "I'm glad I came, too. I'm going to kiss you now. Is that okay?"

She nodded, robbed of speech.

He lowered his head and pressed his lips to hers. Shade's soft lips felt like velvet against hers. His tongue darted out and licked the seam of her lips. She opened for him, and he groaned. His mouth tasted of sweet food and Shade. Her body went lax against him, and he deepened the kiss. Shade let go of her other hand to wrap his arm around her waist and settle on her ass. He squeezed, and she panted in his mouth.

He broke away, his chest heaving. "I need to stop now, or I'll take you right here."

"Okay."

He gave a strained smile. "Okay, what?"

"Take me." Who was this wanton woman?

"Lily…"

Her body went cold and she pulled back as rejection washed through her. How silly of her to think he'd want her. After all, he had been the one to pull away. Even though he'd said he wanted her, it had just been said in the heat of the moment.

"Hey, that's not what I mean." He pulled her close, and she couldn't break away. "I just want to make sure this is what you truly want."

"I…"

"Because I do want it. Bad."

"Oh."

"Yeah, oh. So, you need to tell me what you really want. Because once things start, I won't be able to stop, Lily. You have to be clear."

Her body heated as quickly as it had cooled. They'd just met. How could she feel so strongly about him? "I want you, Shade."

He growled and pulled her close, crushing his mouth to hers. Before she could settle into him, he pulled back.

"Let's back go to your place for privacy. I'm not going to make love to you in public. I don't want to share you."

Lily blinked. She had completely forgotten they were outside where everyone could see them. Wow.

She nodded and pulled out her keys. "I can't believe I did that."

Shade kissed her brow, sending tingles down her spine. "I had forgotten as well. Oh, what you do to me, Lily."

They made it to her apartment and entered her living room. As soon as she locked the door for the second time to make sure it was locked, Shade pulled her away.

"I'm guessing you need to check it at least twice because of your OCD, but is it okay now?" He trailed kisses along her neck, and she tilted her head so he could continue.

"That should be fine." Screw her OCD right now. All she wanted was Shade. A need much stronger than she'd ever experienced overrode all rational thoughts.

"Good." He gripped her ass in both hands and rocked

against her, his erection, long, hard, and thick against her stomach. She moaned, and he swallowed it with a kiss.

Could she come just by his kiss alone? He was sure working on it.

He pulled back and kissed her neck again while removing her coat. Energy rippled through her, and her pulse raced. She ignored the voice in the back of her head telling her that something was different. That her body wasn't feeling everything more, that each kiss, touch, and longing wasn't amplified. Maybe it was just different because it was Shade.

Her body thrummed in a familiar feeling, and she panicked. No, not now. This can't happen now. She stole a glance at her skin and sighed in relief. No ripples. Thank God.

His large palm covered her belly under her shirt, and she froze. She looked into his penetrating gaze and gulped.

"I'm not normally like this, Shade."

"I know; that's what makes you so special." He dragged his hand up and cupped her breast.

She leaned into his touch and lowered her eyes.

"No, keep looking at me, Lily. I want to see your reaction." He brushed a finger over her nipple through her bra, and she swayed in his hold.

"That feels so good, Shade."

"You have no idea how you look right now, your pale cheeks flushed, your eyes bright. You're so responsive. Where is your bedroom?"

She nodded toward the end of the hall, and he brushed

against her nipple again. His eyes were hooded, and she bit back a moan.

"I'm going to make love to you, Lily."

"Now?"

He chuckled deeply. "Yes, now."

"Good."

He removed his hand, and she immediately felt bereft at the loss of contact. Before she could protest, he gripped her ass and lifted her from the floor. She instinctively wrapped her legs around his waist, her core settling against his erection.

He groaned and rocked against her. "What you do to me."

She nodded and kissed his neck, the salty, male taste decadent on her tongue.

He carried her to the bedroom, and she moaned. Oh, God, it was really happening. She was going to have sex with Shade. His hand roamed her back as the other held her firmly in place so she wouldn't fall. She didn't think Shade would drop her. For some reason, she trusted him.

He set her down on her feet at the edge her bed, her body rubbing against him as he did so.

"Lily, last chance. We don't have to do anything you don't want to do."

"I want you. Now."

Shade growled and crushed his mouth to hers while taking off her top. She groaned and leaned back as he lifted his mouth from hers and pulled the top over her head at the same time. He looked down at her and smiled.

"Sit, I want to take off your shoes."

Wordlessly, she did, and he shucked off her boots before running his hands up her calves and thighs until they rested at the snap of her jeans.

She leaned back on her forearms, and he unsnapped her jeans and lowered her zipper. He lifted her bottom and peeled the jeans from her body.

"My God. You're beautiful, Lily." His gaze traveled over her lacy white panties and matching bra. Thank God her OCD compelled her to match all the time.

His hand cupped her, and she arched off the bed.

"I think I want to taste you first to see if you taste like the strawberries I smell on your skin."

Her pulse quickened when he lowered his body flush against hers, his shirt and jeans rubbing against her naked skin.

"I think I like having you almost naked while I'm dressed; it's damn sexy." He unhooked the front clasp of her bra, and her breasts fell, heavy, waiting.

She groaned as he sucked a nipple into his mouth. "I was just thinking the same thing."

He lapped at her breast, then moved to the next. She writhed underneath him as she untucked his shirt so she could feel his skin.

He lifted off her and pinned her arms above her head. "No touching."

"I want to feel you."

"You will, but first I want to taste you."

She moaned and wiggled beneath him. He gripped her hip and kissed her lips.

"I'm going to let go of your hands, but I want you to keep them there, okay?"

She nodded. She'd never done anything like this, but she liked it. A lot.

He released her, and then trailed kisses down her neck, her collarbone, her chest. He tugged at each nipple until she bucked against him but didn't move her arms. She couldn't. She wanted to see what he would do.

He dipped his tongue in her belly button, and she gasped. "Shade."

"Shh, my Lily."

His Lily. She liked that.

He gripped the edges of her panties and pulled them down. She lifted her bottom, and he removed them.

"You're gorgeous." He trailed a finger in her curls, and she blushed.

He lowered his head and kissed her mound. She rocked against him but didn't move her arms. He licked her clit, and she shot off the bed. Pleasure rocked through her as she almost came, but he pulled back just in time.

"I was right; you do taste like strawberries." He sucked and licked her lower lips and clit, and she closed her eyes, not able to take the sight of his dark hair against her pale skin as he went down on her. She'd come right on the spot, and she didn't want him to leave yet.

Selfish, Lily.

Just as she was about to moan for more, he entered a

finger into her, and she came against his hand in shocking heat.

"Shade."

"Look at you go, my Lily." Shade's voice rumbled as she came down from her high. "I've never seen a prettier sight than when you come. Do it again."

He entered a second finger and sucked at her clit as she came again, hard.

When she could speak again, she opened her eyes. "Shade, please."

He stood quickly, removed his clothes, and Lily gawked. Long, lean muscles in honeyed skin. Chiseled pecs and abs with a fine sheen of hair that she wanted to feel against her nipples. His legs were strong and muscled, and his cock…

How would that ever fit?

It was long, thick, and bulging. The mushroom top had a drop of pre-cum that begged for her lips, but she didn't move her arms. Not yet.

"I love the way you're looking at my cock and licking your lips." He leaned down and lifted a condom from his jeans and slid it on himself. "One day, soon, I'm going to have that pretty mouth wrapped around me, but first, I want that pussy around me."

She shivered with need. "Then get over here."

"You were such a good girl and kept your hands up. I'm going to reward you for that."

"Please."

He lowered himself over her, his body heated against hers. His lips claimed hers, and she moaned. He positioned himself at her entrance and brushed a lock of hair from her face.

"Ready?"

"Always."

He entered her, slowly, oh, so slowly. He filled her, and her core contracted around him.

"Oh, God, Lily, you're so tight." His neck strained, and she kissed him at the base of his throat.

"Let yourself go. You won't hurt me. I trust you."

He gave a harsh chuckle. "You have no idea how much I want to, but this first time will be slow. Let's just get to know one another."

When he was fully inside of her, she moaned. "We're about as close as we can get."

He kissed her again then pulled out before rocking back in. Her hips met each thrust until she came again, her body shuddering under his. He rolled until she was sitting on top of him, his cock buried deep within her.

"Shade, I don't think I can come again."

"You can, and you will, my Lily. Ride me."

She placed her hands on his chest while he gripped her hips, and she rode. He lifted up so he went deeper than they had when she was beneath him, his cock reaching that fabled place she hadn't known existed. Her body felt hypersensitive. Every time the tip of his cock hit that spot, tendrils of pleasure wrapped around her, and sped her heart.

"Lily, I'm gonna…open your eyes for me."

She looked down at his fractured blue eyes and came,

her body rolling in heat and energy, his cock twitching as he came deep within her inside the condom. The room glowed in an eerie light. She looked down at her body…

Wait. Was she glowing?

What the hell?

She fell on top of Shade's chest and panted. What was going on? Her body ached with spent need and sleep pulled at her.

She tried to fight it, she needed to know what it was. Why did she glow? Why couldn't she stay awake? Shade rubbed her back and she fell into the abyss, pleased beyond all recognition.

She was his, if only for the moment.

CHAPTER 11

Ambrose clenched his fists as he walked the long golden hallway toward Striker's chambers. He didn't want to be here, but he didn't have a choice. He had lived long enough to know that choices never existed when it came to the council, something he deeply hated.

However, the events that were unfolding did not make sense to him, nor his brother-in-arms, Shade. How had the humans obtained such a large quantity of Shade's dust? Anything over a few specks in one place was unheard of, even for Shade. It was just too coincidental for him that the council happened to find out. Not to mention the file they had on Lily. The angels only had files on humans that may be a threat to the angelic existence. Why had the council found Lily dangerous before this incident? He didn't like it one bit. He had to do an investigation of his own to see what he could do to protect his friend, for Shade was the only thing in his life he had anymore and he could not lose him. The business of this mysterious blue dust made no sense.

How had the council caught word of its presence? Why was one particular member so enraptured with it? Striker was a weasel of an angel and not worth the air he flew in, but he was Ambrose's superior.

Not by power, but by choice. Ambrose had turned down the very seat the brown-winged angel sat upon, a fact that rubbed Striker the wrong way. Well, he supposed that was an upside to this.

He walked into the greeting room and bit back a snarl. The room stank of opulence. It was ornate and gaudy. How on earth could anyone live like this? It seemed to encroach into his space and suffocate him as he ventured farther into the room.

The doors opened, and the gold-robed angel walked through it. Ambrose held back the urge to roll his eyes.

Come on, get with the times and buy a pair of jeans.

Even an angel as old as he tried new things and had given up the idea of robes and the Greek system.

"Hello, Ambrose. Can I offer you a refreshing beverage?"

"No."

Striker stood and waited for Ambrose to say more. That wouldn't be happening anytime soon.

"Well, then. Tell me, Ambrose, why are you here?" He asked as he sat on a throne-like chair in the middle of the room.

Seriously?

"I want to discuss the origins of the dust."

Striker scowled. "You know whom it came from. It is your friend's."

"Obviously, but how did the human obtain it?"

Striker threw up his hands. "How am I to know? It is Shade's fault."

This wasn't going anywhere.

"How did the council come upon the knowledge it had fallen into the humans' hands?"

Striker smiled. "Does it matter? Your *protégé* lost it. It's his job to clean it up. It would be unwise to question the judgment of the council."

Ambrose inwardly scoffed. Shade had done all the work to find out everything he could about Lily, to understand who she was and to do his best not to hurt her. Yet, it was looking like he might have to. Ambrose wanted to know *why* and *how* this had happened.

He didn't trust Striker.

Striker glared. "You better leave now to go help Shade, or it might be too late."

An uneasy feeling went through Ambrose.

"This is not the end of our conversation, Striker."

"I'm afraid it is. Leave."

Ambrose glared but did as he was told. He would be of no help to Shade if he had to deal with the council. What was going on? Something wasn't right, but Ambrose would find what it was, soon.

❄

SHADE LAY BENEATH LILY, HER WARM BODY DRAPED OVER HIM in sleep, his cock still half-hard deep inside her. He looked down at her and brushed the bangs from her face.

God, she was beautiful. He knew that she was attractive, but when she'd lain beneath him, urging him to take her… he'd almost lost it.

Speaking of almost losing it…his wings had almost burst from his back during sex. That had never happened before, not even with Cora. He had thrust into her, and his body had wanted to rejoice and fly. He'd had to flip them so she rode him so his wings would stay put, though the sight of her riding his cock would keep him hard for days.

What had happened when they came? He was pretty sure she'd glowed as she fell on his chest. That wasn't normal. He hadn't slept with a human in many years, but he was pretty sure that, when one of his kind slept with a human, the human didn't turn into a fucking light bulb.

He snuggled closer to her, their bodies entwined in the most intimate of ways. He closed his eyes, contented and slept.

Lily's body twitched, and Shade woke and slid his cock out of her. Before he could shift, her entire body convulsed, her spine arching. The morning sun broke through the room. He could see her body shaking.

"Lily! What's wrong?"

She opened her eyes, and she stared off in the distance with a glassy gaze.

"Lily."

Her body rocked in his arms, and she screamed.

His heart broke as she screamed in pain, tears leaking from her eyes.

"Oh, God, baby."

A convulsion hit her so bad she almost fell off the bed. He maneuvered them until he lay on top of her, holding her down.

"Shh, please stop. I don't know what's going on, so I can't fix it. Lily, wake up, baby." She shuddered below him, her screams lowering to whimpers.

He lifted slightly off her as her movements subsided to dull tremors. A gold dust covered her entire body, as if it were a part of her skin. Her eyes fluttered then her body went limp beneath him.

"Lily?"

He brushed a thumb against her cheek, the gold dust coming off like his own angel dust, but her skin remained a golden hue.

Shade lifted completely off her and almost fell on his ass.

Holy. Shit.

The dust didn't rub off—it was her skin. Her body radiated a warm energy of earth and home...as if the 'real' Lily had been released. She was a brownie, a fairy tale creature that lived in children's books, not real life.

An honest-to-God brownie. How had that happened?

Everything started the click. The storm, her odd energy, the fact that he'd felt drawn to her even though it was against his assignment.

Something had happened to change her from human to a brownie.

The storm. Dammit. He and Ambrose had known something was wrong and lightning had struck *somewhere.* Whatever had happened, it had affected Lily.

The ramification of what this meant to her, her life, her world, and lastly, how it would affect him, made his mind roll. He stood and paced throughout the room.

What was he going to do? How was he going to explain what was going on with her when his whole purpose of being here was to keep all of this shit secret? He was falling in love with this woman, he couldn't just let her fend for herself. She was his—if only for the moment. He'd help her. He had to help her deal with what was to come. This was going to change everything she'd ever known. Her entire genetic makeup had been forever altered, or at least the dormant supernatural DNA had been triggered to react.

Oh, and he'd just had the best sex of his life.

Lily stirred, and Shade went to her. "Lily."

Her eyes fluttered open. "Shade? What happened?" Her voice was hoarse, strained. She rubbed her hand across her face and froze. "Oh, my God."

"Lily, it'll be okay." He grabbed her other hand and sat next to her.

"What do you mean? What's going on with me? I'm gold! Oh, God. I'm a mutant!" She wiggled from his hold, her breasts bouncing against his arm.

This is not the time to get a hard-on, Shade.

"I know you're gold, but it'll be fine."

"Fine? Fine! Is that all you can say? What the hell is wrong with me?" Her body pulsated with energy, and he held her closer.

"Lily, there is nothing wrong with you. You're a brownie."

Oh, good; just blurt it out because that will solve things.

"A brownie? What 's a brownie?" She bit her lip as her eyes fluttered, her mind working over time. She shook her head. "No, I don't care. Those don't exist. I'm sick. You're crazy, Shade."

She pulled from his arms and walked naked around the room. He forced himself not to stare at her curves. This wasn't the time.

"Lily, I'm not crazy. Neither are you. You're a brownie. That's why your skin is gold."

"Just how do you know that, Shade?" She might sound mad, but the quiver in her voice told Shade that she was scared out of her mind.

He stood up and walked toward her. When she didn't back away, he held her close.

"I've known about the supernatural for a while." He didn't want to tell her just how long he'd known and what he was just yet. She had enough to deal with. Honestly, he was scared to death about her reaction.

"What…how…I mean…" Her wide eyes looked ready to storm over and her chest heaved. "And you never told me about the supernaturals? Did you…did you know I was a brownie?"

"No, baby, I didn't know. How was I supposed to bring

the other stuff up in conversation?"

"Am I going to die?"

"No, Lily. This isn't a disease." Well, at least he hoped not.

"How am I supposed to go out in public?" She buried her face in his chest, and he held her closer.

"I'll help you. You can learn to control your powers."

"I don't even know what a brownie is, Shade. Is this a dream?" She closed her eyes and pinched herself. "Damn."

"No, not a dream." He kissed her brow, rubbed the place where she'd pinched herself, and rocked her as they stood naked in her room. This wasn't exactly how he'd imagined their post-coital bliss.

"Oh, God. The storm."

"What do you mean?" He had his guesses as to what had happened to her, but he needed to hear it from her.

She gulped. "It was supposed to be a secret, but considering I'm standing here, naked in your arms and gold, I think I can tell you. The storm a few days ago…was it only a few days ago?" She shook her head, and he kissed her temple. "Lightning struck Dante's Circle and shocked me, my six girlfriends, and Dante. We all were fine except for a few bumps and bruises."

Dear God. He held her close, not wanting to let go. She could have been killed.

"Oh, no! My friends!"

"We'll figure this out. Come on."

He went to her drawers and pulled out a perfectly folded T-shirt and a pair of jeans. He found a matching pair of panties next to its bra and then helped her get dressed. Even though he tried his best to be clinical about it, he still ached when her nipples pebbled as he put on her bra. The goldfish hue to her skin just made her look more beautiful, and accentuated her green eyes. He groaned with desire, but continued to dress her. When she was ready, he pulled on his jeans and led her to her living room. He couldn't think when they were standing next to the bed where they had made love.

He put the kettle on and found some tea bags in her alphabetized kitchen. When things calmed down, he would have to ask her what else she needed done so he didn't mess up her system in the future.

Wait. Future? He shook his head. This wasn't the time to think about that.

"What does this all mean, Shade?" She had sat on the couch and wrapped her arms around her legs, her posture much like the time when he had first spoken to her in the park.

"I don't know yet. No matter what, I'll protect you."

"Protect me?" Her eyes widened, and she paled beneath the gold.

Dammit. He didn't mean to scare her any more than she already was. However, if she was truly a human turned brownie—or an awakened brownie, that sounded better— she might be in danger. Not to mention the fact that the angelic council, if not all the councils, wanted her silenced. Something this big didn't get swept under the rug.

"I only mean to do everything to make sure you're all right," he lied.

She looked into his eyes, and he felt like an ass. "Okay. Shade, this happened after…you know…" She blushed, and he wanted to kiss her again. "Did you do this to me?"

His heart fell to his stomach. "No. I mean, at least I don't think so." For all he knew, it could be his fault.

"What do you mean?"

"I mean that this hasn't happened before. At least, not to me."

"What?"

"I've slept with both supernaturals and humans, but none of them have turned into a new form after sex."

"I really don't want to hear about you with other women right now."

Shade grimaced. "Sorry. Let's just calm down, okay?"

"Calm down? Look at all this dust! How am I supposed to stay clean, keep things clean? It'll get everywhere!" Her chest heaved, and she got off the couch and started straightening the already straight furniture.

He took her hand and pulled her to his naked chest. "Lily, stop. We'll find a way to fix this. I promise."

She shook her head, and he took her lips. She melted into him, and he licked her tongue, loving her strawberry taste. He pulled back and pushed her hair from her face. "Shh, my Lily. We can make you look human. Just think about what you look like normally. Close your eyes. Shh. You can do it."

Lily closed her eyes and let out a whimper then steeled herself. Good girl. He didn't think he could deal with tears right now. Shade leaned forward and kissed her temples, her brows, and then her soft lips. Slowly, she turned back to her human form.

She opened her eyes, looked down, and they both exhaled. "Thank you."

"You're welcome, my Lily." He really needed to stop saying that. As much as he wanted her to be *his* Lily, he couldn't even think about that.

"What are we going to do?"

"I need to go."

"Go?" She pulled back, her eyes wide.

He leaned forward and kissed her nose. "I need to talk to someone who may know more about this, but don't worry. I will be back."

"Can I tell my friends? They may be affected, as well."

Shaded sighed. This was getting more and more complicated, but he didn't see another option. "Yes, but you all must keep this secret. Please. You have to promise me."

She kissed his chin. "I promise. It will just be the eight of us and you."

"Okay, I'll be back as soon as I can." He kissed her again, hard.

When he pulled back, she looked dazed, but he had to leave her before he made love to her again, he had more important things to do; at least that's what he told himself. As he walked out, he looked over his shoulder one more time. She looked fragile, but strong. No matter what happened, she would be all right. She had to be. Shade didn't want to think of another outcome. The green-eyed beauty had already settled into his heart, and he didn't want to let her go.

CHAPTER 12

Later that day, Lily put her face under the spray as she fought to control her emotions. Her pale skin hadn't returned to that gold color, and she could almost think everything was a dream.

She didn't think it was.

She was a brownie.

Whatever that was.

She could have done a search on the Internet, but she was afraid of the answers. What if what she found out said she'd turn into a monster that killed people? Why hadn't she asked Shade exactly what she was? Oh, yeah, she was too busy freaking out over the fact that she was gold. That wasn't like her normally. She usually could step back and look at things analytically, but she couldn't seem to do it then.

What was she going to do?

The water ran down her body, and she finished cleaning before turning it off and wrapping herself in a plush towel she loved. The mirror had steamed up, and she tugged a hand towel across it to clear it away. She'd have to clean it fully later since she'd just gotten towel particles all over it, and it would frustrate her...but what did it matter anymore?

Wow. Talk about an about-face.

Her reflection stared back at her, and she almost didn't recognize herself. Her eyes were bright, and her cheeks flushed. Was it because of the shower? Her new...powers? Or Shade?

With all the craziness over the morning, her moments with Shade hadn't fully settled in yet. Her body still tingled from his touch, and his taste was still heavy on her tongue.

Best. Sex. Ever.

And then she'd woken up, and her body had gone crazy.

It had all been a dream, right?

Not so much.

She pulled on her clothes, made her bed with sheets that still smelled of Shade, and picked up her phone to call Becca. Shade had told her she could tell her friends, and no matter what happened, she knew she'd need them by her side.

"Hey, Lily, how was your date?" Becca said when she picked up.

"Oh, it was great." *Fantastic, actually.* "Can you call the troops and tell them to head over?"

"Is everything okay, Lily?"

She clutched the phone closed to her ear and fought not

to cry. "I don't think so. Just get everyone over here, okay? Bring breakfast."

"You're scaring me, hon. We'll be right over with provisions." Becca hung up, and Lily closed her eyes.

They'd be here soon, and everything would be all right. She swallowed hard and straightened her living room one more time, making sure her pillows were exactly even along the back of the couch.

She went to the kitchen, put on a pot of hot water for Nadie and her tea, and started coffee for the rest of the girls. Then she went to the fridge and pulled out some fresh fruit. She could have made something for breakfast for everyone, but, honestly, she didn't have the energy. Nor the desire.

A sharp knock at the door startled her, and Lily went to open it. Faith stood in the doorway, a disgruntled look on her face and a box of doughnuts in her hand.

"Here." She shoved the box into Lily's hands, walked in the house, and looked around.

"Thanks for coming." She closed the door and locked it twice.

"Where is he? Huh?" Faith snarled. "Did that ass hurt you?"

"What? Oh, God! No! Shade was amazing. This isn't about him."

"Really? Then what is this about?" She folded her arms over her chest and glared.

Another knock at the door saved Lily from having to say anything. She opened it, and the rest of her friends spilled in through the door with food in their hands, kissing her on the cheek.

"Well," Faith started, "Lily says Shade didn't hurt her and he was *amazing*."

"Really?" Eliana asked. "How amazing?"

Lily blushed and bit her lip. "Well..." She so hadn't wanted to divulge her night with Shade with the girls, though that seemed to be the thing to do. She had far more important things to talk about other than Shade's chest, his thighs, his...yeah.

"Tell us!" Becca ordered.

"He took me to dinner." Then he'd made her his dessert.

"And..." Amara urged.

"He took me to dinner and then a walk. Then we came back to my place and..."

"I knew it!" Faith danced around the kitchen. "So how was he? Don't say amazing. We need another word."

"I can't think of anything else." Lily smiled, thinking of the delicate ways he'd played with her body and the way she'd let him.

"Wow. No words, huh? Nice." Jamie squeezed her hand and winked.

"That's so sweet, Lily," added Nadie.

Becca turned a kitchen chair around so she could straddle it. "That's great. Really. But if everything was okay with Shade, then why did you call me and gather us here?"

This was the hard part. How could she break this to them? What eloquent way could she put everything so they would understand?

"Uh…well…I'm a brownie."

And the award for lamest remark goes to… Lily.

The kitchen fell into silence and the girls blinked as one.

"A brownie," Becca said.

"Yes. Last night I turned gold after I woke up, and it turns out I'm a brownie."

"A brownie," Amara repeated.

"Like the dessert?" Faith asked, a twitch on her lips.

"No, not like that. Like a gold woman."

Nadie blinked rapidly and tilted her head. "How much did you have to drink last night?"

"Nothing, I promise. It's true, guys."

Jamie stood and walked over to kneel in front of Lily's chair. "Lily," she spoke softly, holding her friend's hand. "It will be okay. We can get you help."

Lily pulled her hand back and blew her bangs from her face. "Fine. Don't believe me."

"It's not that we don't believe you, dear," Eliana said. "It's just that, I mean, come on, Lily. A brownie?"

Lily shook her head. "I understand." She stood and closed her eyes. Shade had told her to relax and envision herself as a human to become one, so it should work in reverse. Right?

She calmed, ignored the worried mumbles around her and shifted. Her body tingling and rolling with energy —like home.

The girls gasped, and Lily opened her eyes.

She looked at her hand. Her skin was covered in gold dust, and an energy thrummed through her.

She let out a deep breath. "It worked."

"Oh, my God," Faith said.

"Holy shit," Becca exclaimed.

"How did this happen?" Amara asked.

Lily smiled and wrung her hands together. "I don't know. I fell asleep after Shade and I made love, and when I woke up, I was like this." She didn't want to scare them and tell them that she'd had a seizure and felt like her whole body was on fire. No, that part didn't need to come out.

"How did you know you were a brownie?" Jaime asked.

"Shade told me."

"He just knew what that was?" Eliana asked.

"Yes, actually."

"Odd, don't you think?" Faith asked and gave Amara a look that Lily didn't understand.

"Yes, it is. I really didn't have time to think about what all of that meant, ya know. I was a little more preoccupied with being a freaking gold woman. Plus, he said he'd tell me more about it when he got back. He left to go talk to a friend who may know more about what happened."

"Well, we want to know what happened as well, hon," Nadie said.

"I know. We'll figure this out. We have to," Lily said.

"Can you...ya know...." Faith waved her hands in front of her. "I mean, can you turn back?"

"What?" Lily looked down at herself. "Oh, I'm sorry. I forgot." She closed her eyes, focused on being human, and the energy eventually ebbed away.

"That is so cool," Jamie said.

"Maybe." Lily nodded. "I'm a little too freaked out right now to think about it."

"Understandable," Amara agreed.

"So what does Shade think happened?" Nadie asked, and nibbled on a doughnut.

Shit. How could Lily have forgotten the most important part about all of this?

"Well, we think it was because of the lightning."

"Fuck." Faith chugged her coffee and paced around the small kitchen.

"I was afraid you'd say that," Jamie said.

"Does that mean this could happen to all of us?" Nadie voiced the question no one had wanted to ask.

Lily looked around the room at her best friends, each unique and special in her own way. What would happen to them if they turned into something they weren't before? Would it change their relationship forever?

"I just don't know," Lily finally answered. "Shade will be here, and we can ask him."

The girls played with their food, not really looking at one another.

"Whatever happens, we'll stick together. No matter what," Amara finally said.

"We'll kick its ass and find a way to work with it," Faith agreed.

God, Lily loved her friends, but she knew this was only the beginning. What else was coming for them?

CHAPTER 13

Shade walked through the door and threw his keys in the dish in the hallway.

"Ambrose!"

Lily was a brownie. Holy shit. It didn't make any sense. Someone's genetics didn't just change on a whim. How did a strike of lightning do this? There had to be something else going on. A higher power? He might be an angel, but he wasn't one of God's cherubs, if they even existed. He didn't know what else to think. Ambrose would know what to do; or at least help clear Shade's mind from the night before, because, hell, he couldn't quit thinking of that strawberry scent. Damn, that wasn't as important as *why* she'd changed. Fuck.

"Ambrose?" Shade walked to his mentor's room, but it lay empty. Where was he?

A pull in Shade's chest made him draw up short. A

summons from the council again? Damn it. Did they know he hadn't fixed it yet?

Shade cursed. Of course they knew. They seemed to know everything. He froze. What if this wasn't about the dust? What if this was about what had happened to Lily?

The angels had no legal jurisdiction over the brownies. Every species had their own council. They could still use his dust as a catalyst to harm her. He clenched his fists. No, that couldn't happen. He wouldn't let that happen.

The council pulled on him again, and Shade locked his jaw. He would go to them and bow like a good little soldier. But, he wouldn't allow them to harm his Lily; not while he still had breath in his lungs. He looked around the house once more, grabbed his keys, and walked out to the back-yard. His back arched, and his wings unfolded from their hiding place in the pouch in his back. With one last look round him, he shot up into the sky, his rage barely in check.

When he was high enough above the clouds, he closed his eyes and thought of the enclave. His people's world survived in a pocket of space that kept it hidden. An angel only needed to fly high enough and think about it to find themselves there, almost like a transport to their side of the realm.

Shade opened his eyes and flew toward the council chambers. He wanted to get this over with so he could find Ambrose and talk about Lily. He didn't have any time to wait. As it was, he was going to be later than he'd planned in getting back to her. He hadn't called because he didn't want to worry her. Plus, he couldn't tell her about the council meeting.

He cursed and set his feet on the ledge of the cliff heading toward the chambers. What did they want with him? He flexed his wings and walked inside the building, tension coiling through him with each step.

Striker sat on the center seat, his brown wings drooping around him, a smirk on his face. He tapped his fingers against the armrest and rolled his eyes.

Bastard.

Shade looked around the room and came up short. It was just him and Striker. A discreet cough made him turn around to see who was there. Ambrose stood behind him, his arms crossed and a glare on his face.

Odd. What the hell was happening? Striker didn't have the authority to call him in for a meeting like this. It took the whole council, not just one annoying angel, to demand a council presence. Ambrose let out a growl, and Shade arched a brow. Okay…something was going on here.

He moved in position for a fight. If Ambrose was this ticked off, something was wrong.

"Settle down," Striker teased and looked at Shade. "You've failed. She knows. They all know. The girl will have to die."

Shade's pulse quickened. "No, she doesn't know. I still have more time." He clenched his fists.

Must. Not. Punch. Angel.

"Ah, but you don't. You've already contaminated your mission. You've slept with the whore."

How had Striker known this? Had the bastard been watching him this whole time? Without taking a breath, Shade expanded his wings, flew toward Striker, took his sword from its invisible cache—the place all warrior angels had that they could hide their weapons to their body if needed—and held it to the council member's neck. The brown-winged weasel gulped, a bead of sweat running down his oily face.

"*Never* call her that again. Or I will kill you. Slowly." Shade growled, twisting the blade ever so slightly with each sentence.

The bastard tsked. *Fucking tsked.* "I am the council. You have no right to threaten me. I could have your wings for this."

Shade merely moved the blade closer to his carotid artery and raised a brow. "Actually, you are only part of the council. Not the whole of it. If you call her that again, the entire world of angels cannot protect you."

Striker swallowed hard, the movement causing Shade's blade to nick the skin. The angel whimpered, and Shade pulled back. Fucking limp dick.

Shade flew back to the ground, and Ambrose moved to stand behind him. The other angel hadn't said a word during the whole altercation. He hadn't needed to. Shade knew that Ambrose had his back no matter what.

"I'll get the job done. Don't worry. Your precious secrets will be hidden." Shade gave his back to Striker and stormed out of the room.

"I'd watch your little human if I were you, Shade. You

never know what could happen. They are so frail as it is," Striker called out behind him, and Shade fought back the urge to kill him. That wouldn't do any good. Not yet anyway.

"You are lucky, Shade, that you did not kill him," Ambrose rumbled.

Shade stopped and looked at his friend. "Excuse me?"

"You can't kill him. Not yet anyway. He's a council member. Plus, there's something going on that concerns him, I believe. Come. These cliffs have ears."

Shade nodded. "Good, I need to talk to you." The nervous energy flowing through him made him bite off the words.

Ambrose furrowed his brow and nodded. They both lifted off the cliff, their contrasting wings catching a wind draft, and they started home.

As soon as they touched down in their backyard, they tucked their wings away and walked inside the house. Ambrose sat on the ottoman and held out his hand.

"Give me your sword. You got that swine's blood on it. I don't want the damn thing to rust." An avid weapons connoisseur, Ambrose knew all there was to know about swords and other sharp pointy things. It was as much a pleasure for him as it was a necessity.

Shade took his sword out of his cache and held it out. Ambrose shook his head and began cleaning the blade. Shade smiled at the familiarity of the action and went to the fridge to get them each a Coke.

He popped open the top and took a drink, the sweet

taste giving him the jolt he needed. How was he supposed to approach this subject with Ambrose? Yes, he could talk about sex with him; they were past that for God's sake. How did he tell Ambrose that Lily was a brownie? Would he believe him? What would he do with Lily?

Shade shook off that thought. No, no matter what, Ambrose wouldn't hurt Lily; not if he knew Shade's feelings. Right? A sick feeling settled in the pit of his stomach. He didn't want to do this, but he had to complete the assignment.

"Shade?" Ambrose called out from the other room. "What is it you wanted to speak of?"

Shade took another sip of his Coke, grabbed Ambrose's, and walked back to meet him. Ambrose accepted his drink, and he handed Shade back his spotless sword. The blade gleamed like new. Damn, he did good work. Shade could have cleaned it himself, but he was no Ambrose.

Shade sat down and played with the tab on his drink.

"What is it, Shade? Is it about Lily? What does she know?"

Shade shook his head. "Yes, it's about Lily. It's not about the dust. Well, that might play into it later, but no, not yet."

"Okay, then tell me."

"Lily is a brownie. Her skin turned gold, and her body lit up. Her energy is completely different. She's not human anymore."

Ambrose's eyebrows rose. "That's a new one."

"Shit. You've never heard of this?"

Ambrose shook his head. "No, I haven't, but that doesn't

mean it's a unique case. All humans are part supernatural, after all. Their genetics are just so diluted down they've lost all magic. Something must have sparked the change, and whatever supernatural chromosomes she had in the most abundance took over. In Lily's case, it was a brownie."

"That's sort of along the lines of what I thought."

"What do you think sparked it then?"

"The storm."

"I knew that night felt off." Ambrose stood and paced. It was the way his friend dealt with deep thoughts.

"Well, she was struck by lightning."

Ambrose stopped. "And she lived?"

Shade nodded. "Yes, and her friends, as well. I don't know why her friends aren't turning right now. Though, I haven't met them all, so who knows. They could be a new type of shifter for all I know. Dante was also hit, but as he's a dragon, I don't think he would be affected."

"The dragon should be fine. But what of the others?"

He shook his head. "I don't know. Lily has them over now, I believe."

"They'll have to be told."

"I think Lily is doing that."

"You'll have to help and make sure they know the rules of their new society," Ambrose warned.

"I know. I wanted to talk to you first. It was scary as well. I mean, she lit up, Ambrose."

"When?"

"When did she light up?" Shade blinked. "When we were making love."

Ambrose gave a small smile and looked off in the distance. "I think I know the trigger. Not the reason she was struck by lightning, but I have an idea of why she lit up."

"Why?" Shade crushed the can in his hand and sat on the edge of his seat.

"Lily may be your true half, Shade."

His ears rang, and he felt light headed. "Wh…What?"

"Your true half. The one person who is connected to you for eternity. Though I don't know why they call it half because there are triads known in existence." Ambrose looked out the window again, and Shade struggled to breathe.

"But, I thought I had that with Cora."

Ambrose shook his head. "No, neither of us had our true halves. Believe me, we have known."

Shade looked at his mentor as sadness washed through him. So Ambrose's wife, Shade's sister, hadn't been his true half either?

"Why didn't I know about this?"

"Because it was an age-old custom that hasn't been seen in a millennia. From what you are describing, I'm pretty sure that is the case. Congratulations, Shade."

"But she's a brownie, and I'm an angel."

"So? How do you think the lines got diluted in the first place? Angels don't have to mate with only angels. You know this."

He nodded slowly. His true half? Lily was his for eternity. What about the lies he told? Could she get over that?

Should she have to get over a betrayal? Fuck. This whole thing was a mess.

"What are we going to do?" Shade asked.

"You need to talk with Lily. Not to mention these women have a lot to learn. Even if they don't turn, because of their connection to your Lily, they'll have to know. You will have to help them."

"I have no idea how I'm going to do that. I'll figure it out. I have to."

"Yes, you do. While you do that, I need to figure out what is going on with Striker. You do your job and protect the supernatural secret. This whole thing is going to implode. We're going to have to figure out how to teach them and protect them at the same time. Some are not going to be happy that humans can turn. These women are in danger, Shade."

Concern for Lily raced through him. "I'm on it, Ambrose. I won't let them get hurt."

Ambrose sighed. "You are but one angel, Shade."

"And you're another. We need at least to start. Once we do, we can find others to help."

"Good. I need to leave. Go to Lily, Shade. Some-how…"Ambrose squeezed his shoulder. "Lily needs to know the truth. Lies will only harm any relationship you build."

His body tensed, but he nodded. "I know. I'll think of something."

"Grovel if you have to. Don't lose something so precious."

Shade nodded, unable to find the words. Ambrose left

the house, and Shade leaned back in his seat. How was he going to break the news to Lily that she was his true half and that he was a lying ass that had to put his world before her? Well, not anymore. She was his world now, and he'd do what he could to protect it. No matter the cost.

Lily paced in her kitchen, her nerves like pinpricks along her skin. It was later that afternoon, and she was pretty sure she was about to crawl out of her skin; at least that's what it felt like to her. Where was Shade? He hadn't said when he'd be back, but worry had taken over his mind. Was he hurt? What if he'd found out something that would make him stay away? What if he just stayed away because she was a brownie?

Nausea crept through her, and she gripped the back of a chair to steady herself. No. She couldn't think like that. It didn't help the situation. Shade would be back, and he'd have answers. Well, at least he'd be back.

The other women were in her kitchen cooking turkey spaghetti, baking homemade bread, salad, and some kind of dessert. Well, at least most of them. Faith and Eliana were on their laptops researching something at her kitchen table.

No matter what happened in her life, those two were *not* allowed near her stove. Even if they survived the blast, they made more messes than two-year-olds with a box of Sharpies. The other women at least cleaned up after themselves. Lily noticed they were being extra careful today since she was on edge. Oh, she loved these women.

"Lily, I have some bread for you," Nadie said as she walked toward her, a basket of warm sliced bread in one hand and a glass of milk in the other. "You haven't eaten today. And, no, picking at a doughnut doesn't count."

"Yeah," Faith added, "and they were good doughnuts, too. I went all the way to Eli's Bakery on your side of town and bought them myself. All that energy…wasted." She winked, and Lily smiled.

Suddenly, Lily's stomach ached, and she grabbed the roll, stuffed it in her mouth and gulped down the milk without taking a breath.

What the hell?

She slowly lowered the glass and licked the milk from her lips. Her friends stared at her wide-eyed.

"Why…why did I do that?" She blew her bangs from her face and set the empty glass on the table.

"Maybe you were just really hungry?" Nadie offered, though it didn't look as if she believed it any more than Lily did.

Faith tapped some keys on her computer. "Actually, I've read that brownies can be befriended by offering of bread and cream left for them to find. Usually, they like to eat in privacy or in front of family only, rather than in front of other people. Huh. Maybe you think of us as family. Ah, babe, that's nice."

Lily looked at her as if she had two heads. "Where did you find that?"

Eliana smiled. "A website called *Magical Creatures and Beings*."

Lily paled. "Oh, God. So, this isn't a bad dream? Oh, crap. I'd kind of hoped the gold thing was just a figment of my imagination." She plopped down on a seat that Jamie held out for her. "I'm a brownie, and not the cute Girl Scout kind. Oh, God."

Becca smiled and grabbed a slice of bread. "So, I suppose I shouldn't ask if you want to sell me cookies."

Lily growled, her skin turning gold.

The room went silent, and Lily shot out of her seat, waving her arms. "Shit. I'm so sorry, guys. I don't know what's going on with me. I can't control it."

Jamie pulled her into her arms and stroked her hair. "It's okay, Lily. Shade will be here soon, and he'll help you and us."

Faith glared. "Just how do we know that Shade didn't do this in the first place?"

"Because I didn't," Shade growled from the open doorway. He closed the door behind him and walked toward Lily.

Her heartbeat sped up, and she licked her lips.

"You came back." *Great, now I'm sounding like the Beast from the fairy tale Beauty and the Beast.* Her body relaxed, and she faded back to her pale skin.

"Of course I did. The reason you're a brownie is because it's in your genetic makeup."

He took another step toward her, and the women moved to stand in front of her, blocking her from view. *Ah, my misguided and protective family.* Her eyes filled with tears but she blinked them back.

"You need to tell us exactly what you mean. Now," Amara ordered.

The tension rose another degree in the room, and everyone looked ready to spring like a tightly wound coil at any moment. She had to stop this.

She pushed past all of them and walked toward Shade. She didn't touch him but just barely restrained herself. She turned her back to him, this time forming a blockade to protect him. "Stop it!" she yelled. "All of you! This doesn't help anything."

Her friends blinked, their jaws hanging. Lily never yelled. Was this yet another side effect of being a brownie? Or, maybe she was just pissed the fuck off. Yeah. The latter sounded more reasonable.

Lily turned to Shade but still didn't touch him. "What did your friend say?"

Shade brushed a lock of hair behind her ear, and she forced herself not to melt into him. She needed answers. Then she could fall into his arms. Yeah, that sounded incredible. *Focus, Lily.*

"Ambrose agreed with me about the storm." His voice rumbled like a blanket of heat and promise over her sensitive skin.

She wanted to wrap herself around him, rub herself all over him like a cat, then watch as he entered her slowly…then fast.

Who was this woman? Well, she liked her anyway.

"Then does that mean it will affect all of us?" Becca asked.

"I'm not sure," Shade answered. "No matter what happens, you won't be alone. Any of you. That's my promise."

Her friends nodded, still wary.

Nadie wrung her hands together. "What about Dante?"

Crud. How could he have forgotten Dante?

"That is something you'll have to speak with Dante about," Shade answered.

"What?" Lily asked.

"It's not my place to say."

"Okay, Yoda," Faith snarled.

Shade merely blinked, uninterested. *Kind of sexy.*

She let out a breath. It seemed with every answer, twenty more questions popped up. "Fine. Exactly how did you know I was a brownie? I mean, I don't really understand." He'd explained the energy part earlier, but it still didn't make any sense.

"Because of your energy and skin."

"So, I'm a freak."

"No, Lily." He pulled her into his arms and kissed her brow, sending shivers down her body. "You are beautiful. Brownie or human, you are beautiful. Not a freak."

Warmth filled her body as she blushed. Her friends

oohed and ahhed. Well, most of them. Faith and Eliana scoffed.

"Shade…" she whispered.

Shade coughed and looked around the room, as if he just noticed they weren't alone. "I don't know what's in store for you all, but we will figure out."

Every time he said that she believed him. One thing bugged her. Well, more than one thing, but that was beside the point. "Shade, how do you know about the supernatural?" For some reason, the fact that he'd already known about brownies hadn't really shocked her. It made sense that he was one if he knew about them. "Are you a brownie like me?"

Shade laughed softly. "No, Lily. I'm an angel."

She blinked. Well, that wasn't quite what she was expecting. "So, like with wings and everything?"

He smiled and ran a finger down her arm, leaving goose bumps in its trail. "Yes, with wings and everything."

An image of him shirtless with wings as powerful as his body flooded her mind. Sexy as hell. She blushed. She had to remember they had an audience.

"I will tell you more about what I am in a minute," Shade said. "This is where you all need to listen to me. There are, literally, hundreds of supernatural species out there, each with a different society and a different set of rules, but there are some overall rules. Like this must stay a secret. No matter what. You can't tell your families, your friends, the paperboy…nobody."

They nodded. "We understand, Shade. Who'd believe us anyway?" Jamie said.

"When you say hundreds of types of supernaturals, do you mean like werewolves and vampires?" Becca asked.

"Weres, yes, and not just wolves, but no on the vampires." Shade answered.

"So, no Jasper Cullen?" Amara asked.

"I'm afraid not. No sparkly or non-sparkly vampires, and no zombies either."

Eliana furrowed her brows. "But, why not?"

Shade shrugged. "Maybe because vampires are really dead. Supernaturals can withstand much, but once we're dead, we're dead."

Lily's mind rolled. "This is all too much."

He pulled her to his chest, and she closed her eyes. "I know, but you're not alone."

She inhaled his sweet, almost like a luscious chocolate scent, and smiled. "Show me your wings."

Shade pulled back and tilted his head. "Okay." He walked to the center of the room and took off his shirt.

The women gasped and giggled, while Lily blushed watching each muscle on his arms and chest move with a fluid grace.

"Oof," Faith exclaimed.

Lily turned back to her friend, who was rubbing her ribs where apparently Becca, who stood beside Faith, had elbowed her.

"What?" Faith asked and blinked innocently. "He's hot."

Shade shook his head and smiled. His gaze locked with

Lily's and his shoulders twitched. Dark wings came from his back and filled the space around him. Her friends gasped again, this time with awe. The wingspan must have been more than ten feet. Thank God her room had enough space that he didn't knock anything over in the process.

She looked at his wings, and her breath left her. No, they weren't just black; the color was more like an obsidian gleam with shades of indigo woven into the feathers. The tips tapered to a deep, mesmerizing blue.

"Beautiful," she whispered.

"Not as beautiful as you."

She blushed, and some of her friends giggled. Which ones, she didn't care; she was too focused on the sexy angel —yes, angel—in front of her.

"See, Lily? I'm supernatural, just like you. I can and will help you. I promise."

He pulled her into his arms and she forgot everything around them. She could focus only on him and those fractured ice-blue eyes. "I believe you."

CHAPTER 15

Shade drummed his fingers on his jeans as he sat in the car outside Lily's apartment. Why was he doing this again? Oh, yeah, because he was falling for the girl who lived up there, and he didn't want to lose her. He knew it would be over as soon as she found out everything about their past.

He'd gone back to his house soon after showing off his wings to pick up Ambrose's car. Lily had to go back to work the next day, and Shade knew she'd look at that dust and know. She'd probably been too overwhelmed with every-thing else to put two-and-two together, but it was only a matter of time. She already knew about angels…but now she'd discover the true purpose of his being there. It had been a calculated risk, showing her his wings, his dust evident, but she had asked, and he couldn't deny her. He loved the way her eyes had widened, and her cheeks had blushed at the look of him. Call him conceited, but it made him feel like he was on top of the world when she looked at him like that.

But that would change when she found out the truth about his mission; that he'd lied. Would their connection be enough to withstand that? Her self-confidence was already low, though he'd been working on that, now it might break.

So, now he sat in Ambrose's car and tried to gather up the courage to tell her that their meeting hadn't been accidental at all, but instead it was a ruse to earn her trust. He wanted to go someplace nice with her, at least one more time. He couldn't tell her about the dust, not yet. Why? Because he was a coward, that's why. He had tried to convince himself that she needed to know who, and what, she was first, but he didn't want to lose her. That's all it was...an excuse.

Once her friends had left them alone, she'd fallen into his arms and shook with nerves. Then she had told him she wanted to pretend she was normal, at least for one more night. Shade would give that to her, however misguided it was on both of their parts because she was his true half. He could barely wrap his mind around that discovery. There was no way he could tell her that. At least not yet. How could he hurt her like that? Would she ever forgive him?

The lab would be open in the morning, and she'd find out about the dust. Ambrose had wanted to go in and take all evidence away now, but it wouldn't have worked. Lily was too smart for that. She'd put two and two together. Things had changed. Lily was a paranormal as well, and

Shade didn't want to betray her further by stealing her work. Though, in essence, he already had.

He would tell her. Soon.

Shade shook his head. Okay, he needed to get out of the damn car and stop wallowing. God, he sounded like a teenage girl. He rolled his neck to loosen his tightened muscles and headed into the building. When Lily opened the door, Shade almost dropped to his knees.

Dear. God.

She stood there in a red dress that molded to her curves and made him want to peel it off her body…with his teeth. The luscious fabric draped over her breasts and ended at mid-thigh.

He gulped and shifted so his dick wouldn't puncture against his zipper.

Lily raised a brow and smirked. "Something on my dress around my chest area, Shade?"

He looked up and laughed. "You look damned sexy, woman. You know what you do to me." He pulled her into his arms and kissed the side of her neck, inhaling her strawberry scent.

She moaned. "If you don't stop that, we won't make it to dinner."

"I have my meal right here," he growled against her skin, but he pulled back and tucked a lock of hair behind her ear. "I'll be good. I promise."

"Not too good, I hope," she teased.

He groaned. "Woman…" He took her hand and led her

to the car. Once he had her settled, he got in the driver's side.

As he pulled out onto the road, he took her hand. "Is Italian okay?"

"Sounds delicious. So I take it from our last date, and now, that angels eat, right? I mean, you're not forcing yourself to eat or anything because of me, right?" She grinned, and Shade fought off the pang of his lies.

He laughed off his worries. "Angels do everything you do, Lily. We just live a long time."

"How old are you?

"I'm one thousand, give or take a few years. I don't really count anymore."

She didn't say anything, and he risked a look over at her. She sat wide-eyed and he cursed.

"Lily…"

She blinked and smiled. "You just caught me by surprise, that's all. That seems to be happening to me often." She shrugged. "How long do angels and other supernaturals live?"

He rubbed small circles on her wrist and switched lanes. "Supernaturals live forever unless we're killed. Sickness doesn't occur in angels. Some other supernaturals have diseases, but it's rare. I'm not sure about brownies, but it's something we'll have to check."

She sat in silence a bit longer, and Shade got worried.

"That's so long," she whispered.

He pulled into the restaurant parking lot, found a spot, and turned off the motor. He turned to her, reached out and took her hands in his. "It's different than what you've known, but we can get through this."

She shook her head and looked out the windshield. "Why did I want to do this tonight, Shade? Pretend to be normal and go out on a normal date. I'm not normal."

He took her chin in his hands and turned her to face him. "What is normal? You're normal for what you are."

She gave a watery laugh. "I don't think so, Shade."

"Well, your situation is rather unique, but you're still you. That's all that matters, and we'll make it work."

"Thank you, Shade."

"For what?"

"For being you, and for helping me."

He kissed her brow and slid a hand along her back. "Let's go in and eat, okay? We can be our type of normal. Even supernaturals get hungry."

She smiled, and they got out of the car. Inside, the restaurant was nice, with an authentic atmosphere that didn't take itself too seriously. Amara had told him it had the best Italian in the city. Once they were seated, a server took their drink order, and Lily relaxed.

"You really do look beautiful tonight."

She blushed, and he wanted to throw her over the table and take her right there. Probably not the best thing to do in public.

"Thank you. You don't look so bad yourself."

He grinned, and the server came back to take their order. As they relaxed and ate the breadsticks on the table, they talked of movies, books, and other random things they shared in common. He'd say something funny, and she'd throw back her head and laugh. He'd watch the long column of her throat and have to shift in his seat. Seriously, how old was he?

As they walked out the door, Lily commented, "I love that we're talking about inane things."

"I don't think they're inane; I like hearing about you."

She blushed and shook her head. "Well, it's not like we can talk about other things, you know?"

Shade smiled. "We can, just not here." He nodded to a bear shifter who passed them on the street, and her eyes widened.

"How…"

He placed a finger on her lips then kissed her softly. "In the car."

Once inside she turned toward him. "How did I know he was…you know…different? I mean, that he was different. I don't know what he was exactly."

"He was a bear shifter." He smiled at her wide eyes. "It's a feeling you have, right?" She nodded. "It's sort of like an energy that surrounds all of us. Eventually, you'll be able to taste the different energies and differentiate the different species."

"That's kind of cool."

He smiled but shifted in his seat. "Lily, I don't want others to know you weren't always a brownie, at least not yet. Your energy doesn't feel any different than a normal brownie, but I don't want others to know how this came about."

Fear wafted from her, and he rubbed his thumb on her lower lip. "Until we know what we'll say, I just want to be safe, okay?"

"I understand. Can we go back to my place now?"

He smiled and took her hand. "That sounds perfect."

LILY POURED TWO CUPS OF COFFEE FOR THEM AND ADDED cream and sugar to hers. She walked back to the living room where Shade sat on her couch, a grin on his face. She stood there for a moment and just looked at him. Was it wrong that he looked so comfortable in her home?

"Lily?"

She blinked and shook her head. "Sorry, I have your coffee."

He patted the seat next to him, and she smiled. He took his coffee cup from her hands and she settled in next to him. They sat in silence for a moment and sipped the strong brew. It felt comfortable...nice, to have him here. She could imagine them doing this after a long day's work.

Shade didn't live here. She didn't even know where he lived...or what business had brought him here. Was it normal business or the angelic kind? They didn't know enough about each other, and yet she felt comfortable with him. But did she feel comfortable asking about his personal life? That thought made her feel like it was going too fast.

"What's going on in that head of yours?" Shade asked.

She shook her head. He *really* didn't want to know what she was thinking. "Nothing, really."

He took a sip of his coffee and waited.

She let out a breath. "I'm just a little scared, I guess." Well, that wasn't totally a lie. She was scared about what was coming with her own body, her future…and yes, the man sitting next to her. He just didn't need to know that last part.

At least not yet. If ever.

Shade put down his coffee, took the cup from her hand, and pulled her onto his lap. He rubbed small circles onto her back and rested his forehead on hers.

"I know you're scared. If you weren't, I'd be worried."

"I just need to make a list or four, and I'll be fine."

He chuckled against her cheek and she warmed. He leaned closer and kissed her softly, the faint taste of coffee on his tongue.

"God, Lily, I love that about you."

Her heart raced, but she tamped down the excitement. It wasn't as if he said *I love you*. No, that's not what he meant, but it was close enough that tendrils of something she didn't want to think about settled in and wrapped around her heart.

"I do like to keep organized," she whispered against his lips.

"Mmm…" He licked her lips, and she opened for him.

His tongue leisurely explored her mouth as her hands explored him, the panes of his chest, his arms, his neck. She wiggled on his lap, his erection against her bottom.

"You keep wiggling like that, baby, and it'll be over before it starts."

She sighed into his mouth and wiggled again.

He growled and lifted her into his arms as he stood. "Okay, sprite, you've asked for it."

"Sprite?"

"I thought it fit." He smiled and bit her jaw before licking the sting.

She wrapped her legs around his waist and blinked at him. "I like it."

"Good." He crushed his mouth to hers while he walked toward her bedroom.

She pulled back. "Don't drop me."

"Never." He plopped her down on the bed so she bounced.

"Hey!"

"I couldn't resist." He grinned and lowered his body over hers.

Before he could kiss her, she wiggled from beneath him, determined.

"Hey, what are you doing?" He furrowed his brows, and she kissed the line in between.

"I want to try something. Just lie back and enjoy." She lowered herself to her knees, and he grinned like a cat with cream. He folded his hands behind his head and lay back.

"By all means, proceed."

Her hands shaking slightly, she undid his jeans and opened them wide, her breath shuddering.

"Commando?"

He chuckled roughly. "Sometimes."

"I'm one lucky woman."

"No, I'm one lucky man."

She lowered his pants, and he lifted his ass so she could take them completely off over his boots, but the boots blocked her intent. She laughed at the look of a half-naked man in his boots, and he lifted a brow.

"Sorry, I need to take off your boots. I'm not good at this." She blushed. God, how inexperienced could she seem.

He sat up and kissed her, his just-Shade taste settling on her tongue. "I'll take care of it, baby." He quickly divested himself of his boots and shirt, leaving him naked and, by the looks of it, *very* ready for her.

She knelt between his legs and gripped his length. His body bucked, and he hissed.

"Jesus, Lily. I love your small hands on me."

"They look small compared to what I'm holding," she teased as she stroked him.

"Flattery will get you everywhere, darling."

She ran her hand up him again then leaned down to lick the head of his cock. He groaned and she smiled. She loved the power she held over this man, the one with the strength of angels who had the ability to make her knees weak. She was the one making him groan and hiss. She opened her mouth wide and wrapped her lips around his cock..

"Lily."

His heady taste danced on her tongue as she relaxed her throat and took him deeper. His hips thrust slightly, and she held them down while raising her head.

"I'm in charge," she said.

His pupils dilated, the fractured blue of his iris practically non-existent. "Anything."

She gave a coy smile and swallowed him again, her mouth stretching to take his fullness. Her body tightened at the thought of him inside her, filling her. It wasn't the time for that; no, she wanted this to be about him.

She sucked and licked, fondling his balls. His groans grew needy, but he didn't thrust. Good man.

"Lily, you need to stop. I'm going to come."

She just took him deeper, hollowing her cheeks.

"Lily."

With that, he came, his hot seed shooting down her throat. She took every last drop of him before releasing him with a pop.

"That was fun," she teased.

Shade growled and pounced. Before she knew it, she was flat on her back, naked, her legs spread.

"I want you."

"Please."

He wrapped a condom on his still hard length. God, she loved his stamina. He lowered his body then kissed her. Hard.

He pulled back and nibbled her lips. "I can taste myself on you, and for some reason, that makes me hot as hell. You do this to me, my Lily."

He gripped her hips then, in one fluid motion, turned her over so she was on her knees.

"I want to take you from behind, baby. I want to watch the curve of your back as I fuck you. Would you like that?"

She shivered and nodded, too turned on to speak.

His hands delved between her legs, brushing her clit as he dipped into her. "You're wet for me."

"Uh-huh."

"Hold on."

She gripped the sheets as he did her hips before he slammed into her. Her body trembled, and she came. Her nipples hardened to stiff, achy peaks, and she screamed his name.

"Fuck. Your pussy clenched around me in one stroke. I love how responsive you are."

Her body on alert, she pushed herself back to take more of him. He slapped her ass, the sting going straight to her core. He pulled out, then rammed back into her, over and over, fighting to keep his grip as she crested closer to another release.

Just as she was about to come, he pulled out and flipped her so she lay on her back. She whimpered at the loss of him inside her, too out of it for words.

He kissed her lips then slowly entered her again. "I want to see your face when you come, sprite."

She opened her eyes, her gaze locking with his. He threaded his fingers with hers as he slowly rocked against her. Heat built within her until she came against him, his cock twitching inside her as he did the same.

He lowered his forehead to hers, breathing heavily. "I never want to forget this."

What an odd thing to say, but she couldn't say anything back. Emotions choked her as her breathing slowed to normal.

She wasn't just falling in love with this man. She was full-blown oh-my-God in love with him. She barely knew him. He could leave town at any minute, and she was the stupid idiot who'd fallen in love with him.

Damn.

CHAPTER 16

Lily pulled into work, a smile on her face. She'd woken up with Shade's warm body nestled against her back and something hard and ready for her as well. She blushed, remembering exactly how Shade had woken her. She was lucky she'd even made it to work on time.

She'd quickly showered—alone, as the two of them together under the warm spray of water would have resulted in her being late. Shade had kissed her goodbye when he left a few minutes before her, a sad expression on his face. Odd. Maybe he was just as sad to leave her as she was to leave him.

Lily snorted. Sure. Because all males are clingy. As it was, she had to force herself not to act like a clingy girlfriend. That brought her up short. Wait. Was she his girlfriend? Her body tingled at the thought. She wanted that. No, she needed that. She'd always felt so alone, even with her friends. Yes, she'd felt connected to them and they were her family…but it never felt like enough. And, yes, that made her feel selfish as hell. Maybe Shade would help her fill the void. She couldn't rely on that. She'd done that before and look how that'd worked out. She'd dated Bryce, thought she'd fallen for him, even almost married him. She'd left her old job to work with Glenn so she could be near Bryce. Then he'd left her to be with someone prettier.

It was official, with the amount of angst flowing through her, it was high school all over again.

He'd kissed her and said everything would be all right, and it would. Wouldn't it?

So, she was a brownie, a supernatural creature, and she had no idea what it was and what rules and powers came with it. Shade had told her some, and she'd looked up the rest on the Internet. Though she didn't know what she could trust from what she'd read and Shade didn't know the ins and outs of everything in the brownie culture. She didn't have time to stop and think about it, because she had to work. She walked up the stairs toward her office and laughed.

She didn't have to worry about time anymore; that was something she had plenty of now, wasn't it? She'd live for who knew how long all because of a freak storm. Her knees went weak, and she gripped the railing. Her stomach clenched at the thought. What if her friends never changed? What if she was the only one? How would she cope with knowing her friends would die and she would live? Or maybe they'd be in the same boat as her. It was overwhelming. She couldn't think about that now. She had to get through her day and take this new life thing one day at a time. She hadn't been kidding when she told Shade she wanted to make lists. Doing so would calm her and get her mind situated because, right now, between her transformation and Shade, she felt as if someone had put her brain in a blender and turned it on the highest speed.

To top it off, she had to work a job she hated and for Glenn the Sleaze, the boss she disliked even more.

Why was she doing this again?

Oh, yeah, because it was normal, and she needed normal right now.

She reached her desk and paused to take a deep breath. Her skin felt oversensitive, as if the slightest change in temperature or air movement would make her scream. She didn't know if it was because of her night with Shade or her new powers. She worried her lip and tried not to think about it. She had to get through this transformation and learn to be normal, whatever normal was. Nothing had changed. Funny really. For some reason she'd half expected the world to change around her because her own world had changed, but no, her desk was still in the corner, tidy, and in need of a good dusting. Well, at least it looked that way to her.

She put her purse in her drawer and took out a Lysol wipe. She wiped down the top and sides then straightened everything again, making sure the pens were in perfect alignment with the corner of her desk. The action of cleaning calmed her and lifted her spirit some. At least that hadn't changed when her skin did.

Lily looked down quickly at her arms and let out a breath. Still human. Apparently, a stray thought of gold skin didn't turn her gold. Good to know.

"Lily, where the hell have you been?" Glenn demanded from the doorway.

She looked up, her usual irritation with the man bubbling through her veins. "I've been off. Why?"

He glowered, his teeth clenched. "I don't care what you think you were doing, you have work to do here. Do you have that sample done for me yet?" His chest heaved, and his eyes darted from side to side.

Jerk. What was it about that sample that set Glenn on edge and worried her so much?

"I'm having issues with it, but I'll figure it out."

"You better, Lily. You may think you're irreplaceable around here, but remember, techs are a dime a dozen. You're nothing. Get me the results ASAP." He stormed out of her office, leaving Lily with the incredible urge to follow him and kick him in the nuts.

Okay, that was it. She needed a new job. She couldn't take it anymore. Her heart pounded furiously. She had a whole new future open to her, and Glenn and his petty attitude weren't worth it. She wasn't a doormat. First, she'd finish her current project. She wouldn't leave anyone in a lurch even though she wanted to scream and hurt a certain boss of hers.

Putting on her lab coat and walking down to the lab,

determination set in her veins. She'd find out what the heck this sample was and then she'd put in her notice. Yes, that sounded like a plan.

She sat down at the computer and read the readouts from the scan she'd run over the weekend. Huh? Still nothing. What the heck was this stuff?

There were no peaks. Nothing. It was as if she'd run a blank. That couldn't be it. She'd checked it four times and run it twice. Something odd was going on here.

She rolled over to the sample drawer and took out the vial. She held it to the light, and something clicked.

She recognized this dust. It had been on her bed sheets and sprinkled over her body when she and Shade had made love. She'd been too busy enjoying herself to obsess about the dust at the time—something that never would have happened normally.

The dust of an angel.

Shade's dust.

Her heart sped up as a metallic taste settled on her tongue. How did it get to her lab? What would happen if someone found out exactly what it was?

Oh, God.

Did Shade know it was here? She set down the vial and gripped the bench as the events of the past few days ran through her mind. He'd happened to be in the park that day and said he was there on business. Was *she* his business?

Was their meeting and relationship all a lie?

Tears filled her eyes, but she blinked them back. She would not cry over him. She wouldn't. She choked back a sob and put the vial in her lab coat pocket. Then she did something she thought she'd never do as a scientist. She cleared all memory of the data and runs. Then she made sure the rotors, the little cylinders that held the samples, didn't have a speck of Shade's dust in them by dousing them with alcohol and liquid nitrogen.

Even though her heart threatened to shatter into a thousand pieces and her hands shook uncontrollably, she couldn't let this secret get out. It was her world now, even though she felt like someone had torn off one of her limbs.

She went to her desk and packed up her things in a printer box, not taking the care to organize it. That thought almost made her break down right there, but she held herself together. She'd break down when she got home; when she was alone.

She looked around one more time at the place she'd worked for so long and didn't have a moment's loss for it. She'd always hated it. This just gave her an excuse to leave now instead of later. After all, she'd just committed a felony by destroying files and data from a government-owned lab. They might not be watched like most labs, but she'd still get in trouble. She had savings and could find another job in something she actually liked.

"Lily! What the hell are you doing?" Glenn roared.

"I quit."

"You don't get to fucking quit!" Spittle flew from his mouth, and his face turned beet red.

"Actually, yes, I do." She lifted her chin and tried not to let her fear show. She just needed to get out the door, and then she'd be safe. Glenn didn't even know where the sample drawer was. It would take another tech looking around for everyone to realize what she'd done. Frankly, she'd cleaned everything up enough that they may never notice.

She walked past him, and he grabbed her arm, forcing her against the wall.

"Fuck you, you bitch. You're mine. You can't just leave."

Panic seized her for just a moment before her body hummed with energy. She growled and pushed back, her body glowing gold. "Back off, Glenn."

Glenn's eyes widened and he back-pedaled. "You're….you're one of them."

He knew about them? "What do you know?" Was Glenn in on this? Why did he want the dust analyzed so badly?

"I don't know anything, I swear." She narrowed her eyes and he paled even more. "I promise! The guy just came in and said I needed to get you, specifically, to look at it. I swear!"

"What guy?"

"I don't know, but he flew away! Flew! Holy shit. I think I need to sit down."

Bile filled her mouth. "What did he look like?" Please, don't let this be a setup. Why it would be Shade, she didn't know, but already, her heart hurt.

"I don't remember. He had brown...wings...though. Oh, God. He had wings." Glenn crumbled on the floor in a dead faint and Lily relaxed.

Brown wings. So, it hadn't been Shade. Why would an

angel want a lab to know that angel dust existed? She needed to talk to Shade and tell him…but what good would it do? If Shade knew about this, he was using her.

And she'd let him.

Lily kicked Glenn in the shin—*ah, that felt nice*—and his eyes fluttered open.

She shifted the box in her hands and glared. "I'm leaving, Glenn. You can't tell anyone what happened here. Or…or you'll be sorry." Oh, that's just great. What B-list movie could she quote next time? She'd have to work on her delivery.

Glenn nodded, tears running down his cheeks. "I promise. You were never here. I don't know anything about any dust."

Lily nodded. Thank God Glenn was a weasel and easily intimidated. She'd made it to her car and started driving toward home when her adrenaline crashed and her body shook.

He'd lied.

She was sure of it.

No. She didn't know the whole story. For all she knew, it could be a huge coincidence. She snorted and angrily wiped away a tear that had fallen down her cheek. The traitor. There were no coincidences. Not in her world—old or new.

Somehow, she made it home and stumbled inside. She'd quit her job, accidently revealed herself to Glenn, might have found a conspiracy, and Shade might be lying.

All in a day's work.

She set her unorganized box of work things on the floor

by the kitchen door, kicked off her shoes and fell on her couch.

What had she done?

She wasn't impulsive. She made lists of her lists before she made any decisions. Now look at her. Tears streamed down her cheeks, and she choked on her sobs. She promised herself she'd buck up and get over it soon, but, right now, she needed a good cry.

Only ten minutes passed, and a knock at her door brought her out of her misery. Who could that be?

She shuffled over in her stocking feet, trying to wipe the tears from her face, and opened the door.

She bit back a sob.

Shade.

"Lily? What's wrong? Have you been crying?" He walked in and pulled her into his arms.

She stiffened and backed away.

"Lily?"

"Why are you here, Shade?"

He blinked and frowned. "I stopped by your work to pick you up for lunch, but Glenn said you had quit."

She nodded then walked away from him. She couldn't look at those blue eyes anymore.

"What's wrong, sprite?"

"Don't call me that," she spat.

"Lily?"

She went to her coat, pulled out the vial, and threw it at him. "Got something to tell me, Shade?"

He realized she found out the truth about his assignment, and looked at it, shamefaced.

If possible, her heart broke even more.

He knew.

"Lily, I can explain."

"Oh, save it. Just get out. I can't even look at you." She turned, went to her fridge, and then she poured herself a glass of milk.

"It's not how it seems."

"God, you sound like a man caught with his pants down."

"Lily, listen to me."

"Why, Shade? Why?"

"Because I love you."

Her body went numb. "No, you don't get to do that. You don't get to stand there and say you love me to get out of this. You knew, Shade. You *knew* about the dust in my lab. Didn't you?"

"Yes, but—"

"Stop it! You fucking knew who I was before you even came upon me in the park, and I believed that you had met me by accident. I thought you actually saw *me* and not something I could do for you. Oh, God, how stupid you must think I am. I *slept* with you, Shade. I fell in love with you, and all of it was a lie."

Shade's eyes filled with tears as he took a step closer. She felt numb. She couldn't bring herself to care. Their relationship was based on a lie, and that wasn't something she could just get over.

"Yes, Lily. I knew your lab had the dust. That's why I

came here, but you've got the rest wrong. Yes, my job was to find out what you knew, but as I did that, I found out who you were. I got to know the real Lily, and I fell in love with her. All of that is real, Lily."

She held back the tremors and lifted her chin. "How can I believe anything you say?"

He fell to his knees, wrapping his arms around her waist, and rested his head on her stomach. She didn't touch him. Couldn't touch him.

"Lily, you're mine. I hated doing it. *Hated* it, but there was nothing else I could do. I had to put the fate of the angels before my own wishes."

"And, in the process, before me."

Shade nodded and gripped harder. "That ended. I fell for you, Lily."

"I don't believe you."

"I love you. I'd do anything for you. Don't you understand how much it hurt to lie to you? I hated every minute of it, but I had to do it. If I could go back, I'd change it."

"Don't say that. Don't talk to me like I don't know what hurt means. I loved you."

"I love you, Lily. You're my true half."

Something inside clicked, as if a missing piece of her had been found. It was as if she'd finally understood their connection...why'd she'd fallen for him on the spot. Her heart ached to reach out and be with him. "What does that mean?"

"You're my soul mate. The other half of my life. The one I'll spend eternity with."

For just a moment, she let herself picture that future with him. The one with angels and babies and smiles, but that would be a lie. He'd chosen to lie to her and had made love to her under false pretenses. That wasn't forgivable, even to a lonely lab tech like her.

"If that were true, then you wouldn't have done what you did. Leave now." Grief filled her. Grief for a future lost, a love that wasn't mean to be.

"Lily."

"No. Out."

"But, you may not be safe."

"I'm not safe even with you here. You've already proven that."

Hurt crossed his face, but she couldn't care about it. Because if she did, she'd fall to her knees and into his arms. She had to be strong.

Shade rose, a dejected look on his face. "I'll still protect you."

"Find someone else. I don't trust you."

He flinched, and, for a moment, she felt bad, but she had to get him out of her home before she did something crazy like kiss him.

He nodded, trailed a finger down her cheek, and walked out the door.

She watched the door close and held a hand up to her cheek. She could still feel his touch. With a sob, she lowered herself to the floor and wept.

CHAPTER 17

S hade walked into his home blindly. He'd royally fucked up and he had no one to blame but himself. Yes, the council had ordered him to do what he could—anything he had to as ordered—to protect the angels. In doing so, he'd hurt the most important thing in his life.

Had it been worth it?

Hell, no.

God, the look on her face when he'd told her the truth. It had broken him. He'd fallen to his knees and begged her, yet she hadn't wanted to look at him. She'd destroyed him by revealing he'd destroyed her.

Now, she was alone, just like him, and she had no one to protect her.

Shade went to the fridge and pulled out a beer. He gulped it down quickly, letting the liquid help quench his thirst, though he didn't taste it.

He'd lied again.

He wouldn't leave her alone. He couldn't. No, he'd never force her. God, no. He wouldn't let her be on her own with a new and scary world out there. For God's sake, she didn't even know what being a brownie meant!

He took another sip of his beer and sat on the couch, his head in his free hand. How the hell had things taken such a turn?

Oh, yeah, because he was a jackass. Why did he have to lie to her? She'd closed off, her eyes devoid of the warmth he'd fallen in love with. She didn't trust him. The fact that they'd said they loved each other was now tarnished because of his deceit.

He felt worthless.

"Self-pity doesn't help anyone," Ambrose admonished.

Shade glared at his friend and took the last swig from his bottle. "It's not self-pity."

Ambrose raised a blond brow.

Shade cursed. "Fine. It's a little self-pity. Just let me continue for a moment, okay?"

Ambrose leaned back in the armchair. "From the look on your face, I take it our dear Lily found out the truth."

"She's not our dear anything."

"Ah."

"Dammit, Ambrose, I really fucked up."

"Yes, you did. At first, it was unavoidable."

Shade closed his eyes, trying to ignore the pang deep down in his soul. Yes, it hurt that he'd lost something precious. Oh, God, his heart ached, but what was worse was that he'd hurt Lily in the process. That was unforgivable.

"I should have said something sooner."

"Yes, you should have."

"Thanks for cutting me some slack," he said dryly, not believing it anyway.

"Why should I?"

"You shouldn't."

"At least on that we agree."

Shade closed his eyes and pictured Lily's wide green eyes. Damn.

"Once you had developed feelings for the woman, you should have told her, but you were scared."

Shade stiffened, the words cutting deep, but he didn't contradict Ambrose. After all, it was true.

"I left her alone, Ambrose."

"I know. It's something you'll have to rectify. Soon."

Shade looked at the man, a sudden urgency riding him. "What?"

"I've just been to the council."

His pulse thudded in his ears. "The whole council or just Striker?" Fucking brown-winged leech.

"The whole of it."

"And? What did they say?"

"That Lily is a problem that must be rectified."

Shade jumped to his feet. "What do you mean?"

Ambrose shook his head. "They don't trust us to finish our assignment. They've put a hit out on our girl."

Shade saw red, his body shaking. He held back his fists,

not wanted to punch the messenger. "They want us to *kill* my true-half?"

"No, they want someone else to do it. They're sending him soon."

"You've got to be fucking me. What would killing her accomplish?"

"Striker is adamant."

"That fucker wants to kill her because of a speck of dust?"

"And they don't even know yet what she truly is."

"Oh, God. If they found that out…" Shade didn't even want to think about that. What would they do to her if they found out she'd transformed into a brownie? Death might be a kinder fate.

"Shade, we won't let them harm her."

Relief at his friend's words filled him. "So, you'll go against the council with me?"

Ambrose nodded. "I will go up against Striker. I don't believe we know everything, but I do know that he has a vendetta against us both. He must not be allowed to wield this power. I will protect Lily for you and also because she should not die because of the greed and pride of one angel."

"Do you know who they've sent?"

The other man shook his head. "No, but Striker will send them."

"Shit. That fucker is going to have her killed because he wants to get at us. She doesn't know anything she shouldn't because she's a supernatural."

"But they don't know that, Shade. For all they know,

she's a human who's stumbled upon the dust of an angel and is about to go to the nearest news station with her findings or sign a book deal. They're trying to head things off before it gets worse."

"And killing her will stop that?"

"In Striker's mind, yes. He's poisoned the rest of the council with his venomous lies. He wants her dead, and unless we can stop it, he'll get what he wants."

"Then we have to go to her."

"Agreed, though it won't be easy protecting her."

Shade snorted, ignoring the pain settling hard as a rock in the bottom of his stomach. "I don't care what we have to do. She will not be harmed even though she doesn't trust me." Again, he ignored the pain. "I will do all that is in my power to protect her."

Ambrose sighed. "I'm sorry you had to lie to her, Shade."

He closed his eyes, wishing he could turn back time. "Me, too."

They ran to Ambrose's car, and Shade prayed they weren't too late. If she died because of his world, he'd never forgive himself. He'd thought he lost a part of himself when he lost Cora, but his green-eyed beauty just might make him lose the whole of it.

"I WANT HER DEAD! DO YOU HEAR ME? DEAD!" STRIKER SPAT at his second in command, Law.

Law, a gray-winged angel with dead eyes, blinked slowly. "You're telling me this…why?"

Striker balled his fists, rage rising within. "Because it's your job!"

"Uh, no, not so much," Azel, his third, said. The angel flexed his black wings, a bored look on his face. "We don't kill little humans because you can't get the job done."

"You do what I say! I'm the leader." Why didn't they get that?

"We follow you because of your position in the council," Law explained. "You'll get us what we want—the warriors and council dead. Other than that, we're not your lackeys."

Striker paced away. "I need this human dead. It's the only way. With her dead, Shade will fall apart, taking Ambrose with him."

"That doesn't make any sense," Azel said.

"Of course it does. You're too stupid to understand." Shit. Maybe not the best thing to say to two of the deadliest angels out there. These two had been by his side during the Angelic Wars. Their form of torture was legendary, so much so, that Striker had faked their deaths in an elaborate fashion so they could continue their pain play in private. He suppressed a shudder. He *really* didn't want to think about what type of kink they enjoyed.

Striker gave them a brilliant smile. "I didn't mean that."

Please, don't kill me.

Law took a metallic sculpture—a priceless one, though Striker held his tongue—and bent it with one hand. The scraping sound brought bile to Striker's mouth. He could imagine his neck being bent in that same contorted position. Not good.

"I hope you didn't mean that," Law said, his dead eyes boring holes into Striker.

"I didn't. I swear. But...um...where was I? Oh, well, Lily, the human, needs to die. The council ordered it after I pushed. With her dead, they will look toward Shade and Ambrose with disdain and maybe even demote them. Then they'll be easy pickings for you."

Azel nodded, dumber than a bag of bricks. "Fine. Whatever gets us closer to our goal. I'll kill the human. Won't take but ten minutes as long as that ass, Shade, is gone. He is gone, right?"

Striker nodded vigorously. "Yes, I just saw them. She threw him out for good. She'll be easy."

Law cocked his head. "So you say."

Striker spread out his wings and growled. "I'm the leader. You would do well to remember that. Come closer for your reward before we start." The two looked at each other but did as he commanded. With that, he flicked a switch, and the room filled with an electrical charge that struck the two in front of him, strategically placed on metal sheeting in the floor. An angel must do what he could to remain in power.

The other angels screamed in pain and Striker flicked the switch again. "Do you understand me now?"

The others nodded, blood seeping from their mouths. They were too stupid to realize that they could just walk around the setting and not get hurt again. For that, Striker was grateful.

"Good."

"I'll leave now," Azel said, his face not looking so bored anymore.

Striker grinned. Oh, how he loved when things came together. He barely resisted the urge to clap at his good fortune. He must not look like a fool in front of his men. "Good. Now go." Azel left, leaving him in the room alone with Law.

"As for you, Law, I want you to watch the council like you have been." He grimaced at the mention of the elderly busybodies that made up his cohorts in justice. "I want to know their every move. They cannot be allowed to know my plans."

Law nodded. "They won't be a problem."

Good. Plans were in motions. Soon, the girl would be dead, then the warriors. Then he'd be in power. It was all he'd ever hoped to have in his life.

Lily scrubbed the non-existent stain on her kitchen floors, pretending the tears in her eyes came from the ammonia and not the pain in her heart. How stupid could a girl get? She'd slept with a man she barely knew, and she was surprised that things didn't work out?

She wrung out the sponge and set it on the other side of the bucket. Her body felt like it had gone through a week-long bender, and she hadn't even had the luxury of drinking.

She really needed to get over this pity-party, but she deserved at least a few more hours of it. She had almost called her friends, but she couldn't. Faith would say, "I told you so" then go kick his ass, and the others would hug her, bring ice cream, and man bash. Lily wasn't quite there yet.

She drained the bucket, cleaned the sink and removed

her gloves. She grabbed some milk and chocolate and then walked with labored steps to the couch. Sinking into the cushions, she closed her eyes. She'd been craving milk like crazy, but that was most likely due to her new genetics. That was at least something healthy. Who knew what else would manifest itself as she learned what it meant to be a brownie?

Cold crept along her skin. Shade had left.

She couldn't really believe it. She felt numb, as if he'd taken an important part of her when he'd left. No—when she'd made him leave.

Yes, she'd told him, in no uncertain terms, to walk out that door, but part of her had hoped he'd stay.

God, she was a glutton for punishment.

What was all that talk of true halves? For a moment, she'd felt a sense of wholeness when he'd mention it. Then the truth of his deceit had tightened like a noose, and anything warm and good had been squelched.

God, she missed him, and she hated that she did.

Another part of her hated that she hated that she missed him.

A vicious cycle that made her head hurt. A knock at the door startled her. Who could that be? Her heart thudded as a sense of...something washed over her, as if the air had become heavy and charged around her like a sense of danger. Her body turned gold, and her head hurt at the thought of the oncoming threat. How she knew it was a threat, she didn't know. She didn't want to open that door.

"Lily, open the door, dear." A growly voice she didn't recognize penetrated the door, and Lily stood up.

Where could she hide? Did she have enough time to make it out the window? She didn't know, but she needed to get out of there, now.

The door crashed open, splinters spraying around the room, and a chunk of wood slicing her cheek. She winced at the pain and scrambled backward.

An angel walked through, dark black wings unfurled behind him.

Her pulse thudded in her throat.

Shade?

No that didn't make sense. She may not trust him, but she never felt like this around him, not even now.

The man looked up, revealing charcoal black eyes, and a snarl on his face. "Hello, dear. Sorry about the mess. You should have opened the fucking door."

Okay, not Shade.

Lily picked up the nearest weapon , the fireplace poker, and held it in front of her.

Right, like a little metal stick she had no idea how to use could protect her against a who-knew-how-old scary angel with black wings.

She gulped. "What do you want?" Better than nothing.

"It's not a question of what I want, but what I'm going to do."

That didn't sound ominous at all. Damn, the door was the only way out. He had her cornered. Why didn't these stupid new brownie powers help at all? No, she could only turn gold and apparently know when something was dangerous. Like that could help right now.

"You need to go now," She said.

"No, I don't think so." He smiled, and her body froze, a shudder running over her skin.

This was it. She was going to die, and her house was a mess. Right, because that was the most important thing right now. He moved forward, and she brandished the poker. In one swoop, he took it from her hand and threw it across the room. It hit the wall with a crash. She winced, and he growled. Heart pounding, she made a move to run. He grabbed her by the upper arms and shook her. Her head slammed back and forth, and she kicked him in the thigh.

"Fuck, bitch."

She wouldn't go down easy. Twisting and screaming, praying her neighbors would hear, she tried to break free. His hands dug into her arms, and she screamed again. *God, it hurt.* He threw her across the room, her body landing on her glass tabletop that shattered. Shards of glass punctured her skin, sending a feeling of fire through her veins. Tears slid down her cheeks, and she struggled to rise. Her hands crushed into glass, the pieces digging deeper into her skin. She had to get away. If only she could crawl to the doorway...

He pulled her by her hair and dragged her back. A sob clogged her throat as blood seeped down her arms and legs. A deeper cut in her side scared her to death. Oh, God, what had been cut?

Suddenly, she fell back, her head slammed into the floor as the angel let go over her hair.

She heard another crash, a curse, and a groan. She forced open her eyes—when had she closed them? The metallic taste of blood coated her tongue, and she rolled to her side, placing her other hand against her side to control the bleeding.

Oh, God. It was so much blood.

She looked over toward her attacker and let her tears fall harder.

Then she saw Shade.

He'd come back.

Maybe she wouldn't die today.

Shade held a sword, as did the other black-winged angel, who had tucked away his wings. Their weapons clashed, the vibrations making her teeth chatter. Shade pivoted, leaning out of the way of a blow. He bent and shifted, his arm making a slicing motion as the other angel screamed.

Good, he'd cut the bastard.

"Lily, let me help you."

She started and winced at the pain of the motion. She forced herself to turn her head and look at who ever had spoken with that deep, gravelly voice.

"Am...Ambrose." Her words sounded stilted, painful.

"Oh, Lily, I'm sorry we weren't here sooner."

"Help Shade." Here she was, bleeding to death on her floor, her home ruined beyond her OCD repair, and she only cared about the man who'd torn out her heart and stomped on it. Why didn't she just stamp doormat on her forehead? Wow, the blood loss must be making her loopy. That or she was always this sarcastic. Hmm…sleep sounded good right now.

"Lily! Wake up now!"

She blinked and focused on the three moving images of the handsome blond man. Hmm…no wonder Jamie liked blonds.

"I'm sure Jamie has a reason she likes blonds, but that isn't the point right now. You're bleeding heavily, and I need to take a look at it so you can start to heal on your own. By the way, Shade is fine; he's a warrior."

She blinked. "Don't tell Jamie I told you she thought you were sexy, okay?"

Ambrose blushed. Aww, for a stiff guy—snort—he was pretty cute when he blushed. Especially when there were three of him.

"I need to look at the cut on your side now. You're getting pretty loopy, dear."

"Okay, but don't look at anything else, okay? Jamie would never forgive me."

"Okay, Lily, whatever you want."

Lily blinked and looked across the room at Shade and the guy she'd like to kill herself.. Shade had the other angel by the throat, his sword in his other hand and the other angel's sword on the floor. Go Shade.

"Who sent you, Azel?" He pressed the sword closer to the angel's skin, where blood flowed freely.

"Like I would tell you, warrior," he said with a gurgle.

"I won't kill you...yet, but I will make you wish for death."

The other man laughed—laughed. "Don't you know? I like pain."

"Yes, but I know even more ways to inflict pain than you." Shade pulled the other angel to his knees, and stabbed him in the back in swift motions. Black wings shot out, knocking more things from her counters to the floor, forcing her to wince. Shade growled and sliced the black wings from the man's body in two clean motions.

"No!" Azel screamed, his body convulsing on the ground.

"Tell me."

"Who do you think?" the other angel whimpered.

"Striker?"

"Got it in one."

"Do you have proof of this?"

"No, why would I?"

"And no one would believe an angel like you, would they? You're supposed to be dead."

Azel snarled and lifted to his knees again. "I was told to kill the woman so you would die, you fucking bastard."

They wanted to kill her because they wanted Shade to die? How did that make any kind of sense?

She winced as she moved, and Shade looked at her, pain in his features. Before she could blink, Azel leapt on Shade's sword, piercing himself in the heart. Shade jerked and pulled the sword out then placed his hands on the other angel's chest to stop the bleeding.

"Too…late…no…proof…" Azel rasped.

"Fuck. You can't die, you fucking bastard."

"Shade, it's a lost cause. We'll burn the body to destroy the evidence; it would do nothing for the council now. If he'd been alive, he'd have been proof of Striker's deceit." Ambrose deftly bandaged her side and she could feel her skin knitting together on its own, and her headache lessened a bit.

"How…"

"You're a brownie now, Lily. You can heal faster than humans," Ambrose answered.

"Oh."

Shade threw the sword down and ran to her side, his eyes frantic. "Where are you hurt? Tell me. What pains you? Oh, God, Lily, I'm so sorry."

She liked that he took care of the bad guy so she'd be safer. He was a warrior who looked at the threats and then came to her side. Maybe that would prove useful.

"He wanted you," she whispered.

He closed his eyes and set his jaw. "I'm so sorry."

"I'm tired." She pillowed her head on her arm, her body sagging.

He brushed her bangs from her face as she felt Ambrose move away from her. "I'm sorry, baby."

"You're always sorry." That wasn't fair, but she was too tired to care right now.

"Let me take you to my home and I'll help you."

"Are you sure I'm safe with you?" God, she needed to

shut up. Now. He didn't deserve this. After all, he'd just saved her life.

"Lily, I will protect you with my life. I know you don't trust me, but what I'm saying is true. I won't let them come near you. I'm so sorry I was late." He ran an arm down her side, careful of her wounds.

She couldn't let that feel good.

"My house…"

He brushed her hair again, and she closed her eyes. God, she still loved him. That hurt almost as much as the glass. Though that seemed to be healing on its own. So odd.

"We'll fix it."

We. Like he expected to be around.

"Okay. Just take me away, okay?" She just wanted to go to sleep. Or cry. Whatever.

"Okay, baby. I'm going to pick you up now."

She nodded, her eyes still closed. His arms went under her, and he carefully lifted her from the floor. She leaned into his hold and inhaled the scent that was just Shade.

God, she'd missed him.

But he'd lied. She had to remember that.

What a day. She'd lost her job, her Shade, and almost her life. She needed a drink. Or a nap.

Wait…

"Shade." She tried to straighten in his arms, and he stopped.

"What is it, baby? Ambrose is packing you a bag and going to deal with the authorities in case any of your neighbors called the cops. Everything will be okay."

"Oh." Wait, the man was going to touch her panties? Whatever... Other things were more important. "I forgot to tell you with everything else that went on this morning," Shade looked down at her, a broken expression on his face.

She couldn't think about that right now.

"What is it, Lily?"

"I got your dust...like, you know..." She ignored his wince. "And your files and everything. No one will know. Glenn won't say anything even though he saw me turn into a brownie. I know it's not good, but I couldn't help it."

"Lily."

"Wait. The important thing was that he said a brown-winged angel gave him the dust. Do you know what that means?"

"Fuck." His grip tightened, and she whimpered. "I'm sorry, baby." He loosened his hold. "Striker. He's a council member. The same one who sent Azel to kill you. Apparently, he has a death wish. A wish I'll be happy to grant."

"Just don't get in trouble."

He looked down, his piercing blue eyes sexy as ever. "Would you care?"

"No," she lied.

"Let's get you home."

She leaned her head on his shoulder, pain radiating within her body. What was she going to do now? The man she both loved and hated held her in his arms and a dead angel lay behind them. God, when had life gotten so complicated?

She exhaled and bit her lip. Just one more moment in his

arms. That was all she'd take. If she let herself relax anymore, she just might stay. That couldn't happen, not if she wanted to live and be herself. No, she needed to break ties. How? She'd think about it later because he felt too warm to care right now.

Shade set Lily on his couch, trying not to hurt her. Her every wince made him want to fall to his knees and beg for forgiveness…again. He needed to focus on other things right now. Namely, healing his true half and figuring out what the hell to do about Striker.

Bastard.

He fluffed the pillows behind her head and covered her with an afghan from the back of the couch like a regular nurse.

God, the look he'd seen on her face when he'd walked into the room had made the blood in his veins freeze.

Azel had her by the hair, a menacing smile on his face, and a firm grip on his sword. Blood had seeped from his Lily's side and legs. Fury had raced through him at the helplessness he'd felt.

He swallowed hard.

He'd almost lost her, and it would have been his fault. He felt as though someone had thrown him under a bus. There was no denying it. He'd left her alone, and an angel out to get him had almost killed her.

No wonder she could barely stand to look at him. He couldn't even look at himself.

"So, this is your home?" Lily asked from the couch, her pale skin clammy, a side effect of her rapid healing.

Shade nodded. Funny, he'd have thought his first time bringing Lily to this temporary home of his would have been under far different circumstances. He'd known her for what…a week? He held back a sigh. It seemed as though he'd known her for far longer. In essence, based on the way she'd wrapped herself around his heart, he had.

"This is where I'm living now."

Her eyelids drooped but she forced them back open. "I remember you said you were here on business."

That she *was* his business remained unsaid.

He brushed a finger around the healing cut on her cheek, and she didn't move away from his hand. Progress.

"Do you want me to move you to the bedroom?"

She shook her head, pain that she didn't want to lie in his bed slicing at him. He shouldn't think that way though. Maybe she just didn't want to move.

"Okay, then try to rest here. I'll make you something to eat when you wake up. You'll need your strength."

"I could use a bath, too." She blushed, and Shade held back a groan.

He shouldn't be thinking about her naked. Soapy. Wet. That was enough of that.

"After you've rested, I'll get you whatever you need."

"So, is this healing thing normal?"

He gave a small smile and resisted the urge to gather her up in his arms. "Yes, you'll be able to heal faster than a human. It's part of your genetic make-up now, but it takes a lot of energy to do so. Since you're so new at this, your body didn't know what to do, so it healed quickly and, most likely, painfully. So you're going to need fuel."

She nodded. "Eventually I'll learn to control it?"

"Somewhat. I'll help you."

She looked at him, and he could tell she didn't believe that. He bit back a curse. No matter what happened he'd earn back her trust...somehow. He couldn't lose her, not when he'd only just found her.

He let out a breath when she didn't say anything else. "Get some rest, and I'll make you something to eat. Ambrose is cleaning everything up; that's what he does. We have a security system around the place, so you're safe."

She nodded and closed her eyes.

Dismissed.

Dejected, he stood then walked toward the kitchen.

"Shade?"

He turned, his pulse speeding up. "Yes? What's wrong?"

"Thank you." She gave a small smile, and relief spread through him.

Maybe this would be okay.

He went back to the kitchen and pulled out the makings

for a stir-fry. After almost a thousand years on earth, he could cook a decent meal, though he still couldn't cook as well as Ambrose; he could have been a chef in another life.

He took out the wok and heated some peanut oil, the heat feeling good on his cool skin. Then he cut up fresh veggies and chicken and started the rice, tossed garlic and chicken in the wok, then started on the sauce. The room filled with the sounds of sizzling and pops and the scent of stir-fry. He needed to do something mundane while the thoughts in his head warred with one another.

Striker was a traitor.

Fuck.

Shade had always hated him. The ass had never been on Shade's list of favorite people—and vice versa—but, God, to think Striker would stoop so low. To go against the angels was the lowest form of treachery. If Striker had known he was attempting to kill a true half of a warrior…

It was all too much. The idea of a traitor in their midst and a plot he couldn't even comprehend made him want to punch something. Add in his unknown future with Lily and he wanted to scream.

The chicken popped, and Shade stirred and added some rice wine.

Azel was dead, though Shade had thought the fucker had been dead for far longer than that. The other angel had been one of the leaders of the opposing faction in the Angelic Wars. He was supposed to have died. Did that mean his brother, Law, was also alive?

Fuck. Azel's actual death raised more questions than answers.

Who had covered it up? Striker? How long had the bastard been on the other side? Bile filled Shade's mouth. Could it be that the fucking council member was also on the side of the rogues?

He stirred the rice and added the veggies to the wok, glad to have something to do with his hands. All of this had to go deeper than just a vial of dust. Azel had said Striker wanted Shade dead, but why?

Shade's death wouldn't accomplish anything but maybe upset Lily…and Ambrose.

Fuck.

If Shade died, Ambrose would no doubt want justice. If things were in the reverse, Shade would want the same, but if Ambrose went against the council, alone, they'd denounce him. Or worse, kill him. That meant the two top warriors would be gone and Striker would have the ability to take over without opposition.

Holy hell.

It was diabolical. Not to mention fucking stupid. Did the ass really think he could get away with it?

He stirred the sauce into the wok and lowered the heat. He turned off the rice then plated their meal. Lily had only slept a little while, but he knew she needed to eat if she wanted to finish healing.

He set the plates to cool on the kitchen island then poured them each a glass a milk. He'd have preferred a beer, but milk would suit him. His brownie would be craving any type of cream just about now. He held back a smile. Oh, how he wanted to care for her and tend to her needs. If only she'd let him do it on a personal basis.

He walked out to the living room and set the glasses on the table, careful not to wake her. She slept on her uninjured side, her body in the slow rhythm of sleep. Her eyelashes brushed her upper cheeks, long and thick. God, he loved her.

He quickly went back to the kitchen, grabbed their meals, and placed them on the coffee table. The aroma of their food filled the room and his Lily stirred.

"Shade?" she mumbled, her voice low and husky.

He *really* needed to stop thinking about her bedroom voice or anything having to do with sex. She was hurt for fuck's sake. Not to mention she hated him.

"Hey, baby, I made you something to eat."

"I'm tired."

His heart hurt. "I know, but you need to eat and gain your strength. Okay?"

She tried to sit up and winced. He quickly moved toward her and helped her lean against the couch cushions.

She gave a small smile. "Maybe I should have taken your offer of the bed."

Their gazes caught, and Shade gulped.

Bed?

He cleared his throat and handed her the glass of milk. "Drink this. I'm going to clean your cuts. Then we can eat." He sounded like an ass, but he needed to get his thoughts off her naked in bed. Then underneath him. Maybe calling his name as he filled her.

Yeah, because that image was helping.

She took a sip of her milk, handed him the glass, and leaned over so he could access the worst of her cuts. He slowly raised her shirt and cursed. The cut had partially healed, but the wound was angry and red.

She'd have been dead if she hadn't been a brownie. Something Striker hadn't counted on. Thank God.

"How does it look?" she asked.

He gently cleaned around the area, careful not to hurt her. "Healing."

"So, this whole healing thing is a perk." She gave a shaky laugh. "What else do I get? I mean, other than going gold every once in a while, I don't know what special powers I have, if I even have any at all."

He finished cleaning her wound, lowered her shirt, and then handed her her dinner. "First, this is a stir-fry. I made sure you had even amounts of chicken and veggies, so you can actually eat."

She blushed. "Thanks."

"Don't be embarrassed; it's not weird. It's you."

She gave him a look. "It's weird."

"Well, maybe. I'm still okay with it."

She shrugged and took a bite. "Mmm, this is good. I didn't know you could cook."

Pleased that she liked the meal he'd prepared, he smiled. "I've been around awhile, I had to learn."

"I guess you did."

They sat in silence and ate, Shade not really tasting anything he ate. "To answer your question, you'll have strength and the ability to fend off attackers using...I guess you can call it, magic."

She brightened up. "Really?"

"Yep. We'll have to talk to the other brownies to see exactly what it is, but I know you have this sort of energy that you can expel if needed."

"Cool." She frowned and played with a piece of chicken with her fork. "It didn't help too much, did it?"

"Not this time. That's because you don't know how to use it. We'll figure it out."

We? What if there wasn't a we?

Lily set her plate down on the coffee table and blew her bangs from her face. "We?"

He smoothed her cheek, careful of the mark she remembered getting when the door exploded in on her.

"I'd like that."

She closed her eyes, but she didn't lean into his touch. She couldn't.

"I'm so sorry, Lily."

The sincerity in his voice caused a chasm to open within her. She closed her eyes, unable to take it.

"I know you are, Shade."

"When I first came here, it was to protect a secret bigger than me. I didn't know you, had never even set eyes on you, but then I met you. Each time we spoke I fell that much further in love and felt like that much more of a bastard for what I might have to do." He took his other hand and rubbed small circles on her wrist, sending shivers down her spine. "I hated it. Hated it, but when we kissed, I knew I had to tell you."

"Then we slept together, and you still didn't tell me."

He nodded. "I know. I was a coward. I didn't know how to broach the subject. No matter what, I would have fought for you. I *have* fought for you with the council, even before you became a supernatural, Lily. I would have done anything, and now that you're a brownie, it was all for naught."

She closed her eyes. She'd been so angry, so lost, when she'd found out. Even then she'd known he didn't have a choice. It didn't make it any easier to swallow though. She knew he loved her, as she did him.

She opened her eyes, and his fractured blue eyes bored into hers. "I can forgive you, Shade. I don't know if I can forget."

Relief washed over his face, and she almost broke down and threw herself into his arms. Only the pain in her side and the fact that she had to be stronger than that held her back.

He leaned forward, his lips pressing softly against hers. She sucked in a breath and closed her eyes, her resolve weakening. He was so gentle, so caring, even when he'd been the worst sort of ass.

He pulled back, and she relaxed, though she missed him.

Traitorous body.

"I need to know more about you."

"Anything," Shade agreed.

"Who are you?" She blushed. "I mean, what do angels do? What is their purpose? Or really, what is yours?"

"I'm a warrior angel. I protect the other angels and dole out justice."

"But who decides who and what is just? God?"

Shade shook his head. "No, we're not God's angels. We're just another race. The council decides what is just. There are three sects of angels. The council, which is a group of elder angels who are our leaders. The warriors, which is a small group of us who are stronger than others who protect our race. Then the others. Though they are still strong and important. Without them, we wouldn't have a race. They are the reasons we are alive. They are our teachers, healers, philosophers. Angels didn't come into existence to oversee humanity. We came into being because we were one of the original supernaturals. We were the ones who went into hiding first. We were the ones who formed our council first, though I don't know if that did any good. The council members aren't the nicest of angels."

"We live our daily lives either in our enclave, which is a special hidden part of our world where we congregate. Other species have similar places. Some angels go out into the world and live amongst the humans, but not all. I live in the enclave, but I still move among humans because I crave it. I enjoy learning new things and evolving as times change. Not all angels do that, but I'd like for them to. It's enriching.

Angels also mate with other species, just not humans. Our lifetimes are just too different for that to be feasible."

"Wow. So, you're not just a normal run-of-the-mill angel. You know, if angels were run-of-the-mill."

He smiled. "Not quite."

"Is that why Striker wants you?"

His face clouded over and he snarled. "Yes, and I believe there's more, but I have to prove it."

"I can talk to someone about what Glenn said if that helps."

He relaxed and took her hand. "If it does, I'll let you know. I still don't want Striker knowing about you and your new self yet. Okay?"

Right. Because everything she did apparently turned into danger.

"So, you're a warrior who enforces the law, so you have to uphold it."

He nodded.

"That's why you did what you did." The pieces began falling into place.

He kissed her palm. "Yes, but that doesn't make it right."

Her skin tingled where his lips contacted her skin. She reached up and brushed his cheek. His body was warm and inviting. "I will find a way to trust you again, Shade. After all, saving my life should help out some."

Their gazes connected, and he traced a finger over her lips. "I never want to see you hurt again."

Daringly, she leaned forward and kissed him lightly. "I

need to know more about what *I* am, so I can find out what *we* are."

"I'll do anything."

"I know."

Bacon sizzled in the pan, and Shade flipped over each of the strips. The aroma of eggs, bacon, and hash browns filled the kitchen, and his stomach rumbled. Lily sat on a stool beside him as he cooked. She'd refused to relax anywhere else. He didn't mind. He liked having her near, not only because he loved the way she looked in old jeans and one of his button-down shirts, but also because the dangers that surrounded them weren't gone just because he wanted to live in this too-homey atmosphere. No, for all they knew, Striker, and even Law, could be on them any moment. However, Shade didn't think so. Striker would need time to regroup after losing Azel.

"So, sprite, are you ready to learn some more about what you are today?"

Since she'd said the night before, she wanted to know who she was before she could find out who they were as a couple, he'd oblige because it was fine with him. He'd give her a jumpstart on her education.

Her eyes brightened, the rosy color that had been absent from her cheeks the day before, back.

"Of course. What do you have for me?"

"Well, in folklore, brownies are useful house sprites, which mean they assist in tasks around the house." He grinned as recognition dawned.

"My cleaning."

"Yep. You've always had a predisposition toward having things in order. That must come from your genes. At least partially."

"Does that mean all brownies are OCD like me?" She grinned.

"I think you're one of a kind."

"Jerk!" She batted him with a dishtowel, a smile on her face.

"Hey, I meant it in a good way."

"Sure."

Brave, he leaned down and kissed her. When she didn't pull back, he took it as a good sign.

"And," he continued, "they are usually good natured, but mess with one of their friends, and you better watch out."

Lily tilted her head, a thoughtful look on her face. "I could see that. Though, how I could protect anyone is just a guess."

He plated their food and walked with her to the table. As they ate, he reassured her. "We just don't know your trigger, but we'll figure it out and then learn how to control it. That's why we're going to meet the brownies today."

Her eyes widened, and she choked on her eggs. He pounded on her back and gave her some water. "I'm sorry."

"It's okay. You just startled me. So, we're telling everyone?" Fear clouded her eyes, and Shade felt like an ass for bringing it up like that.

"I think we at least need to tell the brownie council. They aren't as, well, stern as the angelic council, and they'll know how to help you. The more I think about it, the less I think we can hide this. There are seven of you that could, or have already, changed. Who knows what your friends will turn into? I don't know why they haven't turned already, there must be a trigger we're not thinking of. We need answers. I'm not knowledgeable enough about the intricacies of brownies to help you with every detail."

She played with the food on her plate, lost in thought. He lowered his fork and clasped her hand. "I won't let them harm you."

Her gaze caught his, and he fell that much more in love with her.

"I know."

Relief spread through him. At least she gave him that much, although he hadn't protected her the day before because, he'd left her. He clenched his fists and held back his rage. He wouldn't do that again unless he had someone watch her. He loved her too much for that.

"Okay, tell me something else about what I am."

He nodded. "Okay, well, brownies are very loyal to their families."

A shadow passed over her eyes, and he felt like an ass all over again.

"What is it?"

"Nothing."

"It's something. Tell me."

She shrugged and took their dishes to the kitchen. He followed and helped her dry as she washed them.

"I don't really have a family."

"Maybe not blood relation, but you do have your friends." *And me.*

She smiled. "Yes, you're right. I mean, my parents are alive, but not really parents, you know? They're just people who I used to live with even though they gave birth to me. I haven't really talked to them since I broke up with Bryce." She scrubbed the pan harder.

"Bryce?" He held back the jealousy dripping off his tongue.

She looked up at him, surprised. "Oh, my ex."

"I gathered that."

She laughed. "He's not worth mentioning. Just an ass that I thought I'd fallen for, moved across the country with, and then lost when he found a stacked blonde."

"What a bastard." He'd have to look up Bryce and kill him. Okay, maybe just maim him.

"Yeah, pretty much. He's balding, married, and has three kids that he hates according to what people tell me."

"I guess you lucked out."

She looked up at him and smiled. "Yeah, I guess I did."

He couldn't take that for more than what it was. Though he hoped it was so much more.

Once they were finished, Lily changed clothes into a sundress, though Shade missed his shirt on her small body. They got on his bike and rode to the edge of the forest. His erection dug into his zipper at the feel of her body wrapped around him, but he did his best to ignore it. Today was supposed to be about her and not his urges.

Yeah, it was going to be a long day.

He pulled over, and they dismounted. As he put away their helmets, she wrung her hands together and stared at the tree line.

"You ready to go?" he asked.

"No. Yes. Maybe." She laughed, and he pulled her into his arms. She wrapped herself around him, and he inhaled her sweet strawberry scent.

"We don't have to go in."

"Yes, we do."

He kissed the top of her head, and she moved away. "Okay, then. It's not that far in."

"How do humans not see it?"

"It's like the angel enclave where I live." Her eyes widened at the mention of where he lived and he inwardly cursed. They had a lot to discuss. "There's a pocket of space between two trees where a whole word lives."

Her eyes widened. "That's not possible."

He stopped and kissed her nose. "I have wings, baby; anything's possible."

"It doesn't make any sense though."

"Lily, physics tells us that multiple dimensions can exist. Humans just haven't proved it yet. If they'd ever think past string theory and quantum dynamics, they'd understand. Well, I'm going to prove it to you now."

"This is kind of cool."

"Yeah, pretty much."

"Lily Banner, welcome home," said a voice from beyond a copse of trees, making both of them stop in their tracks.

"Shade…"

"It'll be okay." He took her hand with his free one, ready to reach for his sword if he had to fight.

"You won't need that, young man." A small female, a brownie, with long brown hair and warm eyes walked toward them, and Shade immediately felt at peace. It was as if this woman meant no harm, even if she could have brought it. This woman would make his true half happy. That much he knew.

He nodded, and Lily gripped his hand tighter.

"Thank you for bringing our Lily back, young Shade Griffin. It's lovely to finally meet you, Lily dear."

"What do you mean?" Fear and anticipation laced her voice.

"It was told to us many centuries ago that a lost child would be brought to us by a blue-eyed warrior with a lightning-quick determination. Welcome home."

"You knew this would happen?" Shade asked.

The woman shook her head. "No, not quite like this. Once the storm approached and you consummated your binding, we knew Lily was ours." They both blushed at the mention of just how they'd consummated. "Silly me, I forgot to introduce myself. I'm Agda, the brownie council leader."

Lily bowed her head, and Shade followed. Power and warmth resonated from the leader. This brownie was no weakling. Brownies are fierce warriors, and it would probably be best to give her proper respect.

"You know me?" Lily asked.

"Of course, child. As brownies, we're connected and can feel each other. Though you're still so new, you may not notice it yet. But, you will. We will always be here if you need us. Come and meet some more of your family. Shade, you are welcome, as well. You are family now that your true half is with us."

Lily's grip tightened on his, and she looked up at him. Moisture filled her eyes, but she smiled. "I'm home."

He kissed her cheeks and brushed the tears from her lashes. "Yes, you are."

"Come with me?"

"Always."

They met the rest of the council and various others. There were brownies everywhere, young, old and new, like her. The brownies were tall, short, and all sizes in between, as unique and interesting as every species imaginable. Each home was a rounded dome set between two trees or rocks, the front doors wooden with vines of ivy decorating the outside.

The people wore clothes mostly brown in color, and the fashion was a mix of the past with the present. Some wore garb that looked like robes, while others dressed in jeans and T-shirts. Truly eclectic, but fitting. Each brownie would come up to them smile, hug, and touch. They were truly a warm race.

They loved his Lily because she was one of them, and for that Shade knew he could trust them. After all, they were her family. Distant family, yes, but family. They ate around a fire in the center of town, the group coming together in a party to celebrate the return of one of their own. They roasted a large pig on a spit and had every type of bread and cream he could think of, and there was music and dancing.

Shade laughed when he noticed a few of them counting the veggies and pieces of cheese on their plates to make sure they were even.

"You're not alone," he whispered and cuddled her close.

She smiled, her body glowing gold with peace. "I know. I'm so happy right now."

He kissed her softly and met Agda's eyes. She smiled warmly, and Shade nodded. This woman understood his Lily, and for that he was grateful.

A young male brownie, who appeared to be about ten years old, walked up to them, his body gold, and a small smile on his face.

"Lily? Would you dance with me?" The boy darted a glance at Shade as if asking permission.

"Oh, I don't know the steps." Lily burrowed into his side and Shade kissed her temple.

"Try it out, baby. I'm sure he'll take care of you."

Lily kissed his chin then nodded to the boy. "What's your name?" she asked.

"Timmy. And I promise to take good care of her." He held out his hand and Lily walked to the circle that surrounded the fire and danced to the music performed by the brownies.

"You love her," Agda said as she sat near him.

"With everything I have."

"Then take care of her. We'll always be her people and be here if she needs us. But she belongs by your side."

Shade nodded, his gaze not straying from the green-eyed beauty as she laughed and danced.

"Good. Then I can let you leave with your neck intact."

Shade laughed. "You know, even a warrior like me knows when to be fearful."

Agda patted his hand as if he was ten years old, not a thousand years old. "That's why you've made it this far. Smart cookie." She walked away and Shade turned his attention back to his Lily.

Afterward, they walked back toward his bike. Conversation was easy. She bounced as she told him of the brownies she'd met even though he'd been by her side the whole time. God, she looked beautiful with a smile on her face. Their fingers intertwined, she leaned into his side, and he let out a sigh. He could almost forget the world around them and the dangers that lurked. Almost.

"Shade, before the sun goes down, will you take me flying?" Lily asked, surprising him.

He stopped beside his bike and rubbed a thumb on her cheek. "Now?"

"Please? If it's not too much trouble." She grinned and kissed his jaw.

"Sneaky, sprite. You're buttering me up."

She licked his ear, and he groaned. "Yep. Is it working?"

He caught her lips and kissed her hard. "Yes," he said when he pulled back breathless.

She smiled, and he took off his shirt. "Sexy."

He grinned. "Good to know." He let his wings emerge, the feel of them sliding and stretching was like breathing fresh air.

Her hand came up to touch the wings, awe on her face. She pulled back, and he grabbed her hand. "Touch me." *Everywhere.*

Her fingers danced along the edge of his wing and trailed down. He bit back a groan.

"Does that feel good?" she asked.

"Almost too good. You'll need to stop, or I'm going to bend you over that bike and show you how good."

Her eyes widened, but she didn't pull back her hand. "Maybe next time."

His cock hardened almost to the point of pain. Fuck. He gripped her waist and shot up into the air, startling a squeak out of her.

"Shade, don't drop me." She wrapped her arms around his neck but still looked at the ground, a smile on her face.

His arms tightened, and they flew higher. "Never."

She wrapped her legs around his waist, her core directly on his cock. "Shade."

"I have an idea," he growled. Cautious of the air draft he glided in, he trailed his hand around her panties and touched her core. Wet.

"Up here?"

He kissed her neck, and she arched against him. "We'll have to be careful, but we'll be fine."

"I trust you."

Hope and need warred within him. Trust. She trusted him. He kissed her and dropped a few feet. Her scream caught in his throat.

"Undo my pants, but don't let them fall past my ass. That wouldn't be good."

She laughed and did as she was told. His cock fell into her palm, and she squeezed.

"Fuck, don't do that or it will be over before it's begun."

She laughed and held onto his back pocket.

"Dammit, I don't have a condom." Disappointment ran though him.

"It's okay; I'm on the pill."

"Thank God." He lifted her slightly, moved her panties to the side, and filled her. Bare. Silk. Hot. Need. Goodness.

All his.

"Shade."

"Lily."

He dipped lower in the air so she slid off his cock slightly. She clenched around him, and she smiled. "Don't leave me."

"Never." He arched back up in the air fast, the momentum forcing her on his cock, hard. They gasped and he smiled.

"Do that again." She moaned.

"Oh, I plan to." And he did. Over and over again, until the both came in a sweaty tumble of wind and limbs. He lowered them to the ground near his bike, and he slid out of her.

"Oh, my God. We'll have to do that again." She stood on wobbly legs and tucked him back into his pants.

"I like the sound of that."

He put his shirt back on, and they got on his bike and headed home. They'd needed that. A moment to themselves. The world would come at them soon, but for now, they had each other.

He pulled into his driveway, and they went back inside.

"I should call my friends."

"I already did."

She stopped and turned toward him. "When?"

"While you were sleeping. Faith almost killed me through the phone, but I told them you were okay and that I'd take care of you."

"They believed you?"

He nodded. "They didn't seem to know what had happened yesterday morning."

She shook her head. "That's between us."

He kissed her softly. "I'm sorry, Lily."

"Stop apologizing. Just don't lie to me again."

"Okay." He brushed a finger down her neck.

"Okay? That's it?"

"You're my true half. I don't need anything else."

"Okay, we need to talk about that. I mean, I don't know about you or your family. Talk to me." She furrowed her brow and he kissed the line it made.

He let out a breath, sat, and pulled her onto his lap. "What do you want to know?"

"Tell me about your family."

He rested his cheek on her head. She had to ask that, but it was past time he told her. "My family passed away during the Angelic Wars."

"The what?"

"The Angelic Wars. A faction of angels tried to break off and control our brethren, thereby humanity." One sentence to describe centuries of pain and loss? How trite. "If they controlled the angels, they could control humanity by destroying it."

"That's horrible."

"My parents died early on in the war, but they had long, enriched lives."

"That doesn't make it hurt any less."

She kissed his jaw and he closed his eyes.

"I also had a sister," he said, his voice gruff.

"Had?"

He nodded. "She married Ambrose."

Lily held his face in her hands, her large green eyes filled with tears. "What happened to her?"

"Ambrose and I were off at another battle, when a group of rogue angels went to Ambrose's and killed Ilianya, my sister, and their two children. She was pregnant at the time." Pain sliced and clawed at him. Tears threatened, but he held them back.

"Oh, God, Shade." She kissed him, tears running down her cheeks.

"I wasn't there, but my fiancée, Cora, was." God, why hadn't he been there?

"Fiancée?"

"Cora didn't make it either." Images of her broken body filled his mind. Blood, glass, rocks…everything.

"Oh, Shade. I'm so sorry." She held him, her body his support as he fought for strength.

"Ambrose broke down and hasn't been the same since." His friend hadn't laughed or truly smiled in years. While Shade had put on a facade, Ambrose had just shut down.

"What about you, Shade?"

"What about me?"

"What about your feelings?"

"I'm fine," he lied.

"No, you're not."

He kissed her, but she pulled back, sorrow on her face.

"How do you know me so well?"

"Because I just do."

He looked off into the distance. "They were so small, Lily. How could someone hurt such innocent people like my sister and her children?"

He closed his eyes, his body shuddering at the onslaught of memories. He'd been the one to find them. The children on the ground, his sister covering the smallest one with her body. Cora on the ground, reaching for the other.

Gone.

Lily, her body warm against his, held him while he broke down.

"I'm used to being the one consoling," he rasped out.

"That's why we're a team."

He chuckled wetly. "I like that idea."

CHAPTER 21

"Why didn't you tell me?" Jamie asked as she paced in Shade's living room.

They'd called her friend over that evening because Lily couldn't be cut off anymore. She needed her friends or, as Shade had put it, her family. They were her lifeline. Of all her friends, Jamie was the most like a sister. Plus, she'd already told the other woman a lot about Shade. As soon as they'd called, Jamie had run over and wouldn't stop pacing.

"I'm telling you now," Lily answered.

Jamie let out a breath and plopped on the couch. "That doesn't really answer my question."

Lily sat beside her friend and wrapped an arm around her. "I'm sorry. Everything happened so fast, and then I needed time to absorb it all."

Jamie leaned closer. "Fine. Don't let it happen again."

Lily grinned. "I promise, if a rouge angel attacks me, I'll call you the second I can reach a phone."

"That's not funny!"

"All I can do is laugh about it. If I didn't, I might go a bit crazy."

"So, Shade's taking care of you?"

Lily warmed at the thought of her blue-eyed angel. "Oh, yes, he is." She blushed as Jamie gave her a knowing look.

"Oh, do tell."

"Shade is…well, he's…"

"Did I hear someone call my name?" Shade came from the back of the house, a cocky grin on his face.

Damn, those super-hearing ears of his. Freaking angels.

"Go back in your room. Lily was just about to dish on you."

"Jamie!"

"Yes, Jamie, I would suggest you let your friend off the hook." Ambrose's deep voice startled them, and they looked back at him. "I already have to deal with sleeping in the next room. I do not care to listen to their sexual exploits again."

"Ambrose," Shade growled.

Ambrose merely raised a brow. He pulled the axe from around his back and sat. Jamie gasped, but Ambrose polished it, unconcerned.

"You have an axe," Jamie stated.

Ambrose blinked, and Lily bit back a grin. She'd only known the angel for a little while, but she already knew he was a supernatural of few words and a large weapon collection. Odd how the sight of a large weapon didn't freak her out so long as the weapon was in his hands. Talk about life changes.

"Observant."

"Stop acting like an ass, Ambrose," Shade scolded.

Ambrose lifted his other brow. How did he do that?

"Do you usually carry large pointy things around like that?" Jamie asked.

"Yes."

"Talkative, aren't you?"

"I'm a regular old chatter box."

Shade let out a laugh. "Was that a joke, old man?"

"Perhaps."

"You did it again," Lily teased.

"Don't count on it happening again," Ambrose said.

"Of course not," Jamie agreed.

"Well…" Shade froze, his body tense, a frown on his face, and the room quieted. "Lily, take Jaime and stay behind Ambrose and me at all times." He tossed her a set of keys. "Go if I tell you. Take Ambrose's car."

"What's going on?" She walked to him.

He crushed his mouth against hers, the urgency of it sending tremors of fear down her spine. He pulled back and brushed her bangs from her face.

"We've got company."

"Do you know who?"

"No, but they're getting closer."

She nodded and pulled Jamie to her side.

"What does he mean, Lily?" Jamie whispered.

"I think Striker, that angel behind this, may be coming.

I'm not sure, but whoever it is, isn't our friend."

"I believe it's Striker." Shade looked down at her, and her breath caught. "I will protect you."

"I know."

Ambrose raised the axe he'd been polishing, a cold frown on his face. "They're here."

A crash from the front of the apartment made the blood in Lily's veins freeze. Shade and Ambrose would protect them. If all else failed, she'd figure out how to find her strength. Hopefully.

A metal canister rolled into the room, and Shade yelled, covering Lily's body with his. The canister exploded, sending a dust that smelled of sulfur through the room.

"Shit, demon's dust." Ambrose growled and fell to the floor.

"Demon's what?"

Shade coughed, blood trickling from his mouth. "I'm sorry."

Her pulse raced. "Shade! Oh, God." Jamie ran to Ambrose's side. The other angel lay on his back, blood pooling around him from his pores. Lily held Shade's head in her lap, tears running down her cheeks. Was he dead? She felt for a pulse, her body relaxing when she felt the faint flutter.

"Oh, he won't die…yet." A man walked into the room, an even scarier looking man trailing behind him. "It's demon's dust, made up of one hundred bodies of demons burned alive. Very rare, and very potent."

"You must be Striker." Her voice didn't betray her fear;

good for her.

"In the flesh. I'm sorry that our first meeting will also be our last. Don't worry though. Your death will help us all." He gave a laugh of pure menace. "Well, at least it will help me."

The other man cleared his throat and glared at Striker.

"Oh, and, of course, my friend, Law, here."

"I am not your friend."

Striker let out a breath. "Fine. My ally, Law, here. Better?"

"No."

"Whatever. We're here to kill the girl." Striker turned to Jamie and tilted his head. "Kill the spare woman first then this one will feel distraught over it. Then kill her."

Law raised his brow. "Is that all?"

"For now."

Law smiled and pulled a sword out of who knew where and stalked toward Jamie. He lifted the sword, and Jamie screamed before ducking.

"Bitch!"

"I'm not going to sit here and die for you!" Jamie ran to the kitchen while Lily lifted Shade from her lap to chase after them. Jamie lifted a butcher knife and held it in front of her.

"You think that can best me?"

Lily picked up a stool and smashed it across Law's back. The angel—no, boulder—didn't move. *Shit.* Law turned and pushed her across the room, her back crashing hard against the wall in the dining room off the kitchen. Pain ricocheted up her arm, and she saw it sat at an odd angle. Her body rolled, and she almost vomited. Not again. She didn't want to die. She staggered to her feet, her vision blurring.

Jamie screamed from the kitchen. Her body lay on the floor, blood pouring from her side. Lily took a step toward her. She had to save her friend. A hand pulled her back against the wall, and she cursed at the pain.

"Stupid bitch," Striker growled. He slapped her across the face, the sting nearly blinding her. "You don't get to help that little one in there. You get to sit here," he pulled her hair and forced her head to the side to watch Jamie try to crawl away, "and watch your friend die. To be sure you can't move…"

Sharp. Hot. Pain.

Something silver dug into her side, she couldn't see what it had been, and a warmth seeped through her shirt. Her body swayed, but Striker held her up. Law raised his sword, toying with her friend. Jamie tried to crawl away, but Lily didn't think she would make it.

Rage bubbled up through Lily. It was as if she'd finally unlocked something. Energy pooled through her as her body strengthened. Her body glowed gold, radiant.

This was her true self.

She growled.

Striker pulled back, but still kept his hand on her. His face lost all color and he blinked. "What the fuck are you?" Striker yelled.

She pulled from his grip and knocked him back with amazing strength. With determination in her step, she walked toward the kitchen, picked up Ambrose's axe that lay on the floor next to his motionless body, and growled again.

Law paused in mid motion, his sword in the air about to decapitate her friend, looked over his shoulder, and Lily struck. She cleaved his body in two at the neck, his head rolling to the ground, his body standing for a few moments before it crumpled to the floor. Blood seeped around them, and Lily dropped to her knees, the last of her energy gone.

"I'm sorry, Jamie," she rasped out.

Blood trailed from her friend's lips as she tried to smile. "You look good in gold."

Lily rested her head on Jaime's cheek, their tears mixing with their blood.

"You stupid bitch! You killed him. I don't know what the fuck you are. You can't be a brownie because you were a fucking human, but you're going to die now."

Striker swung his sword then stopped mid motion. A thin line of blood appeared at his neck.

"No…" Striker whispered, his eyes wide.

His head slid off his shoulders, and Lily gasped. Shade leaned against the wall behind Striker's dead body, his face ashen, blood leaking from his mouth, eyes, nose, and ears.

"Lily."

Her spirit broken, her body in pain, tears rolled down her cheeks. "Save Jamie."

Ambrose came into the kitchen, a look of sorrow on his face. "I will try."

"It's pretty bad." Jamie coughed, blood coming out of the

corner of her mouth.

Ambrose knelt by them and ran a finger down Jamie's cheek. "Don't ask questions, but you will live."

Confusion covered Jamie's face, and Lily felt the same. "Ambrose…"

"I said no questions." He gently picked up her friend, wincing as he stood, and carried Jamie away.

"Lily, let me look at you." Shade walked toward her, and she met him halfway, sliding in the blood of their enemies and each other's.

"I thought you were dead," she croaked out.

He brushed her bangs from her face with a bloody hand. "I'm okay." He winced. "Well, I will be. He didn't have enough of the dust to do permanent damage."

They staggered to the living room and collapsed. "Where did he get the dust?"

Shade shook his head and took off his shirt. He placed his wadded up shirt on her wound, and she winced.

"Sorry, baby. I need to get the bleeding stopped so you can heal on your own." He kissed her, blood and all, and she melted.

She'd almost lost him.

"I don't know where he got the stuff, baby, but we'll find out. It doesn't matter. We're alive and there will be hell to pay with the council, but we'll make it through."

"Will you be in trouble for killing Striker?" If so, that didn't make any sense. The other angel was a traitor and a murderer, but did they have proof?

"I'll get out of it." Though he didn't sound too sure.

"I love you," she whispered.

He held her face in his palm and rubbed a thumb over her bottom lip. "I love you, too."

"Don't leave me," she begged, uncaring of how she sounded. She couldn't lose him.

He gave a sad smile. "Never."

JAMIE HAD PASSED OUT WHEN AMBROSE CARRIED HER TO HIS room. He cleaned her wounds, ignoring the odd pain in his heart at the thought of this girl—no woman—hurt. She wasn't a supernatural. Not yet, anyway.

Whatever the lightning strike had given, it hadn't manifested in her yet, if powers manifested at all. He suspected it would take Jamie meeting her true mate and consummating the relationship for that to happen.

He knew for a fact that wouldn't happen. It couldn't.

And, because of something that he couldn't tell her, much less himself, he could help her heal her wounds. They would ask questions, but that didn't mean he had to answer them. That was something left for later… or never, if he had anything to say about it.

He didn't have answers anyway.

At least not any he wanted to give.

He bent over her and healed her side. The wound knitted together, and she sighed. He healed her other cuts and bruises, and an unexpected connection formed between; a bond that could not be denied. them

"Ambrose?" Jamie turned her head and opened her brown eyes.

His breath caught at the beauty, but he shoved it away. He'd had his chance at a happy ending. He didn't need another.

"What is it, honey?"

Honey? She wasn't his honey. His honey was long since buried. A dull pain throbbed where his heart used to dwell.

He didn't like this brown-haired girl. She brought up too many memories of a life he'd rather forget.

"Thank you."

A strange feeling filled him, much like... hope?

He shook it away.

"Do your best not to get stabbed next time." He stood and turned his back, hating that he felt like an ass.

Jamie coughed from the bed, but he forced himself not to turn back. "You know me, always falling onto sharp, pointy things. I'll be more careful."

"Do."

Ambrose walked out of the room, ignoring the pull to make him go back.

Jamie would be fine, and he could ignore her. He had other things to do anyway. Like figure out how they'd explain Striker's death to the council. He needed proof of the angel's traitorous acts.

He set his jaw, determined. Shade would not pay for another's acts. The younger angel was like a brother to him. He couldn't lose him.

Because if he did, he'd have nothing left.

CHAPTER 22

A summons from the council never led to good things. Shade walked through the ornate hall, his fists clenched. The death of a council member couldn't go unnoticed, as much as Shade would have liked to sweep it under the rug. Literally, in Striker's case. As soon as he'd ensured Lily was healed, he'd felt the tug of a summons.

He'd kissed her softly, though she'd done her best to hold onto him. She had known as well as he did, that the council would not be happy. He would do his best to get back to her. He'd just found her. He didn't want to leave her yet, or ever.

His body still ached where he'd healed from the demon's dust. Fuck, just one whiff of that stuff could kill an angel. Thankfully, Striker hadn't had enough for two, and he and Ambrose were warriors, though it'd almost killed him to feel helpless, then watch as Striker attacked Lily.

His Lily had done incredibly well as a warrior. She'd found her trigger and fought back. Even though the caveman inside him wanted to lock her away to keep her safe, the fact that she had the strength to take care of herself brought more pride than anything he could have done to protect her. He'd have done anything to avoid taking a life, even the life of an angel as horrible as Law. The look on her face...

She'd killed Law. He'd help her pick up the pieces for what she'd done, just as he knew she'd do for him. She wouldn't face the consequences of that action because, according to the council, Law was already dead.

It was only the death of Striker for which they had to answer.

Shade was ready. He'd do whatever he could to go back to his Lily.

He walked through the doors that reached to the sky, and Shade couldn't help but remember the last time he'd been summoned to a full council. That event had led him down this strange path and to her, and it had been worth it in all respects.

He just had to live through this meeting

"Shade Griffin, you've decided to grace us with your presence," Caine drawled, his eyes narrowed.

Shade bowed his head. "You've summoned me."

Caine lifted a lip in disgust. "You've killed a council member. Do you understand what you've done?"

Shade met the other man's gaze. Caine flinched and

Shade inwardly smirked. "I killed a traitor and a murderer. I've done our race a service."

"You killed an angel in cold blood to protect a *human*!"

"That *human* is my true half, and I expect you to treat her as such."

"A human cannot be a true half."

Shade closed his eyes. The truth would come out sooner or later, but he couldn't have the council think he'd hidden anything.

"She *was* human. Not anymore."

"That's not possible."

"Actually, it is. A lightning bolt struck, awakening something in her DNA." He was careful not to reveal just how many had been struck.

"Lightning, you say?" Agnes, another council member, asked.

Shade nodded.

"It doesn't matter; she will have to be killed. We cannot allow abominations in our midst," Caine spat.

Rage filled Shade, but he held his ground. He was in enough trouble as it was.

"Caine, I'm disappointed in you," Agnes said. "Lighnting is from the gods, or our God, as you'd put it. It is a blessing." She leveled her too-knowing gaze at Shade. "A blessing that must be handled with careful hands, but I'm sure you and your mentor are doing just that."

Shade gave a quick nod, relieved.

Caine threw up his hands. "Fine. Let Ambrose deal with the *blessed,* but it's a moot point. Shade, you're the reason we're here. You killed a council member, and you have no proof of his so-called crimes."

Shade growled. No, of course, he didn't have proof. He wasn't allowed to search Striker's home as he was the murderer in the council's eyes.

Agnes gave him a look of pity, but she didn't say anything. He clenched his fists. They wouldn't kill him, would they? He'd fight his way out if he had to do so.

"Shade Griffin, for your crimes against the angelic council and all they govern, I sentence you to a life on the ground. You're to lose your wings."

Fuck. No.

Caine flew from his seat, sword in hand. "Kneel and take your punishment, traitor."

"Is this how you reward someone who saved your life?" Shade asked, ready to flee if he had to. He didn't want to kill his way out. He just wanted to get back to Lily and keep his wings. Each was such an integral part of him. He wouldn't be himself without them.

"You killed a man who did more for this council than you ever have."

"Now that's a lie," Shade growled.

Caine raised his sword, and Shade tensed.

"I would refrain from doing that if I were you, Caine," Ambrose said from the doorway.

Shade's body relaxed somewhat at the sound of his friend's voice. The other angel had found something. After all, the council had only barred *Shade* from Striker's residence, not Ambrose. Ambrose may have been there, but he hadn't laid the final blow. There was no such thing as guilt by association by angels. If they killed then they also were killed. Hopefully, just not this time.

"You were not invited to our chambers, Ambrose!" Caine bellowed.

Ambrose raised a brow, cool and collected. "I see. Since when was it in the best interest of the council for a warrior to be tried and convicted without counsel?"

"Since he killed a member of our council and doesn't deny it!" Caine screamed.

"Of course I didn't deny it. I only deny the reasons you think I've done it," Shade argued.

"Ah, yes. Those reasons." Ambrose hurled a gold-plated book at Caine, who dropped his sword caught it.

Shade stood, the last of the tension leaving his body. That book must be the proof they needed.

"What is this?" Caine asked.

"Your proof," Ambrose answered.

"And? It's a book."

Ambrose let out a sigh, and Shade held back a laugh. "If you would open the book and read it..." Shade bit his tongue. "The book clearly states all of Striker's exploits. Like how he gave the dust to a human man named Glenn. You see, Striker wanted to find a pretty woman who didn't have a man in her life so that Shade might fall for her. Honestly, it was such a stretch that I'm surprised it worked. How he wanted me and Shade dead. Oh, and how he was the leader of the rogue angels in the Angelic Wars."

The other council members let out gasps and Shade

wanted to scream. Really? He'd already told them all this, yet they hear about it from a book and now they believe? Yes, it had been written in Striker's hand, but he'd have thought that, after having fought for them for a thousand years, he'd at least have earned a fraction of their trust.

Apparently not.

Caine cursed and leafed through the gold-plated book. Gold-plated? Really?

"Striker was an arrogant and stupid man to have left this around."

Ambrose grinned. "Indeed."

Caine closed his eyes, and Shade waited. "In light of these new developments, I rescind the order to take your wings, Shade."

Shade waited again.

Caine cursed. "Fine. I apologize."

He nodded. "Forgiven, but remember, the lightning-struck victims are mine." He'd told the women he'd protect them, and he would.

"Agreed. Take care of them. Not all will be as…lenient as I am." Caine walked away and Shade held back a snort. Yes, others might want to hurt the women, and that's why he and Ambrose would protect them.

Caine turned back. "Oh, it seems we have an open seat on the council. Do either of you want it?"

"No," he and Ambrose said quickly.

Caine threw back his head and laughed. "Didn't think so. Oh, and Shade, congratulations on your true half."

Shade smiled, thinking of his green-eyed beauty. He was

going home to his Lily and was keeping his wings. What more did he need?

He and Ambrose walked outside, the wind in their hair. "Thanks, old man."

Ambrose smacked him on the back, careful of Shade's wings. "Anytime. Now, I do believe the girls are at Dante's Circle. Should we head there?"

"About time."

LILY LEANED INTO SHADE'S SIDE AND SIGHED. IT WAS OVER, AT least mostly. She still was a bit OCD, but she could at least control it better now that she'd accepted her powers. Shade was safe from the council, and so was she, come to think of it. She snuggled closer to Shade, his freshly cleaned smell soothing her. He wrapped his arm around her and kissed the top of her head.

"Hey, you okay?"

"Mmm hmm."

He grinned and bent to capture her lips. She sank into his taste as if she would into the most decadent chocolate she could buy.

"Uh, enough with the PDA already," Faith said, interrupting them, she threw a pretzel from a bowl on the table.

"What did I say about throwing food?" Dante asked, then sat, straddling a chair at their table.

"That we shouldn't do it with you not around?" Nadie asked, batting her eyelashes.

They broke out into laughter, and Dante rolled his eyes, taking a sip of his beer. They'd closed the bar and gathered at their usual table, drinking their usual drinks and having a most unusual conversation.

"So, you're telling us that the reason we were all struck by lightning was because the gods, or God, wanted to awaken something in our DNA?" Becca asked.

Ambrose nodded. "Either that, or it's nature's way of bringing forth more supernaturals."

"So, we just have to have sex with our true half, and *bam*, we're growing horns or wings?" Amara asked, playing with her glass of rum and Coke, but not drinking.

Lily blushed and hid her face against Shade's side. Her friends laughed good naturedly, but God, talk about mortifying.

"That's what we think," Shade answered, laughing.

"Don't laugh at me," Lily pouted, holding back smile. He was just too cute for his own good.

"I'm sorry, baby." He kissed her again and she forgot what she was supposed to be mad about. He was particularly good at that.

"I'm glad you're okay though, Jamie," Nadie said. "I don't know how you healed so fast, but maybe it's a good thing everything is changing."

Jamie gave a small shrug and darted her gaze to Ambrose, who pointedly ignored everyone at the table. Whatever had happened in Ambrose's room when he'd healed her had made them both act oddly, but Jamie wouldn't spill. Whatever it was, Lily was glad that her friend had healed, though the question as to how danced on her tongue.

"Well, I don't think any of us are feeling any different. So, maybe nothing will happen," Eliana said, looking hopeful.

"I don't know," Lily countered. "I started feeling different once I met Shade in the park."

"Yeah, because he was hot," Faith said.

"Thanks, dear," Shade teased.

Faith saluted him with her glass and took a drink.

"Faith?" Lily asked.

"Yeah?"

Lily leaned into Shade and narrowed her eyes. "Mine."

Faith threw back her head and laughed. "He's all yours, dearie. I don't need a man."

Shade tugged her closer. "I like when you're all possessive."

She smiled up at him. "I just wanted to make it clear."

He kissed her again, and Dante threw a pretzel. "Get out of here if you're going to do that. Some of us like to eat in peace." He darted a glance toward Nadie, but she wouldn't look at him.

"You threw food!" Lily laughed.

"It's my bar and my prerogative. Now get lost."

Shade stood and took Lily with him. "Sounds good to me."

"I guess I'll see you guys later. Just be careful, okay? If you start to feel funny or full of energy, let us know. Because that means you might have met your true half." She waved bye and stole a glance at Jamie, who had lowered her head, her skin pale.

Huh. Her friend was hiding something.

"Let it go, sprite." Shade kissed her temple and walked her to his bike. Mmm…his bike.

"I just want to know what's going on with Jamie," she said while he put on her helmet.

"You will." He adjusted the straps and kissed her nose.

"I love you, Shade."

"Marry me."

She froze. "What?"

He cursed. "Damn, I was going to wait until we drove to the forest to meet the brownies to ask. You just look so cute with your little helmet on, I couldn't help it."

"Did you just ask me to marry you?"

Shade shuffled his feet, looking uncertain. "Yes?"

"We've just met." But something inside clicked. He was hers as she was his. Oh, she loved this man and wanted to for eternity.

"I know, but we're true mates. I know that doesn't mean anything to you yet, but it does to me. Lily, I want to see you when I wake up every morning and make love to you before bed and in the middle of the night. I want to plan our lives and show you the world. I want to see you grow round with our young. I want to see our babies grow up and have babies of their own. Please, Lily. Marry me."

Tears streamed down her cheeks, and she jumped into his arms. "Yes!"

He caught her and held her tight. "Oh, thank God. I was so afraid I messed it up."

"Well, maybe you should have let me take off the helmet because I look like a dork, but I think you did perfectly."

He grinned and kissed her. She wrapped her body around his, ignoring the catcalls of her friends. They must have heard her scream. Shade's warm body surrounded her, and she finally felt at home. Maybe a strike of lightning wasn't so bad after all.

The End
Coming soon in the Dante's Circle World, Her Warriors' Three Wishes.
Ambrose's story.

A NOTE FROM CARRIE ANN

Thank you so much for reading Dust of My Wings! I do hope if you liked this story, that you would please leave a review! Reviews help authors and readers.

Dust of My Wings started the Dante's Circle series for me and it was a fantastic time to write. I not only got to start a new paranormal world—something I love to do—I also got to look into a little more science. For those of you wondering, yes, each lightning struck woman will get a book. In fact, you can read them now! I'm also not telling you what they each turn into. So check out the books in the Dante's Circle series!

Thank you so much for going on this journey with me and I do hope you enjoyed my Dante's Circle series. Without you readers, I wouldn't be where I am today.

If you want to make sure you know what's coming next from me, you can sign up for my newsletter at www.CarrieAnnRyan.com; follow me on twitter at @CarrieAnnRyan, or like my Facebook page. I also have a Facebook Fan Club where we have trivia, chats, and other goodies. You guys are the reason I get to do what I do and I thank you.

Make sure you're signed up for my MAILING LIST so you can know when the next releases are available as well as find giveaways and FREE READS.

Happy Reading!

Carrie Ann

Dante's Circle Series:
  Book 1: Dust of My Wings
  Book 2: Her Warriors' Three Wishes
  Book 3: An Unlucky Moon
  The Dante's Circle Box Set (Contains Books 1-3)
  Book 3.5: His Choice
  Book 4: Tangled Innocence
  Book 5: Fierce Enchantment
  Book 6: An Immortal's Song
  Book 7: Prowled Darkness
  The Complete Dante's Circle Series (Contains Books 1-7)

Carrie Ann Ryan is the New York Times and USA Today bestselling author of contemporary and paranormal romance. Her works include the Montgomery Ink, Redwood Pack, Talon Pack, and Gallagher Brothers series, which have sold over 2.0 million books worldwide. She started writing while in graduate school for her advanced degree in chemistry and hasn't stopped since. Carrie Ann has written over fifty novels and novellas with more in the works. When she's not writing about bearded tattooed men or alpha wolves that need to find their mates, she's reading as much as she can and exploring the world of baking and gourmet cooking.

www.CarrieAnnRyan.com

Montgomery Ink:

Book 0.5: <u>Ink Inspired</u>

Book 0.6: <u>Ink Reunited</u>

Book 1: <u>Delicate Ink</u>

Book 1.5: <u>Forever Ink</u>

Book 2: <u>Tempting Boundaries</u>

Book 3: <u>Harder than Words</u>

Book 4: <u>Written in Ink</u>

Book 4.5: <u>Hidden Ink</u>

Book 5: <u>Ink Enduring</u>

Book 6: <u>Ink Exposed</u>

Book 6.5: <u>Adoring Ink</u>

Book 6.6: <u>Love, Honor, & Ink</u>

Book 7: <u>Inked Expressions</u>

Book 7.3: <u>Dropout</u>

Book 7.5: Executive Ink
Book 8: Inked Memories
Book 8.5: Inked Nights
Book 8.7: Second Chance Ink

Montgomery Ink: Colorado Springs
Book 1: Fallen Ink
Book 2: Restless Ink
Book 3: Jagged Ink

The Gallagher Brothers Series:
A Montgomery Ink Spin Off Series
Book 1: Love Restored
Book 2: Passion Restored
Book 3: Hope Restored

The Whiskey and Lies Series:
A Montgomery Ink Spin Off Series
Book 1: Whiskey Secrets
Book 2: Whiskey Reveals
Book 3: Whiskey Undone

The Fractured Connections Series:
A Montgomery Ink Spin Off Series
Book 1: Breaking Without You

The Talon Pack:
Book 1: Tattered Loyalties

Book 2: <u>An Alpha's Choice</u>

Book 3: <u>Mated in Mist</u>

Book 4: <u>Wolf Betrayed</u>

Book 5: <u>Fractured Silence</u>

Book 6: <u>Destiny Disgraced</u>

Book 7: <u>Eternal Mourning</u>

Book 8: <u>Strength Enduring</u>

Book 9: <u>Forever Broken</u>

Redwood Pack Series:

Book 1: <u>An Alpha's Path</u>

Book 2: <u>A Taste for a Mate</u>

Book 3: <u>Trinity Bound</u>

<u>Redwood Pack Box Set</u> (Contains Books 1-3)

Book 3.5: <u>A Night Away</u>

Book 4: <u>Enforcer's Redemption</u>

Book 4.5: <u>Blurred Expectations</u>

Book 4.7: <u>Forgiveness</u>

Book 5: <u>Shattered Emotions</u>

Book 6: <u>Hidden Destiny</u>

Book 6.5: <u>A Beta's Haven</u>

Book 7: <u>Fighting Fate</u>

Book 7.5: <u>Loving the Omega</u>

Book 7.7: <u>The Hunted Heart</u>

Book 8: <u>Wicked Wolf</u>

<u>The Complete Redwood Pack Box Set</u> (Contains Books 1-7.7)

The Branded Pack Series:
(Written with Alexandra Ivy)
Book 1: Stolen and Forgiven
Book 2: Abandoned and Unseen
Book 3: Buried and Shadowed

Dante's Circle Series:
Book 1: Dust of My Wings
Book 2: Her Warriors' Three Wishes
Book 3: An Unlucky Moon
The Dante's Circle Box Set (Contains Books 1-3)
Book 3.5: His Choice
Book 4: Tangled Innocence
Book 5: Fierce Enchantment
Book 6: An Immortal's Song
Book 7: Prowled Darkness
The Complete Dante's Circle Series (Contains Books 1-7)

Holiday, Montana Series:
Book 1: Charmed Spirits
Book 2: Santa's Executive
Book 3: Finding Abigail
The Holiday, Montana Box Set (Contains Books 1-3)
Book 4: Her Lucky Love
Book 5: Dreams of Ivory
The Complete Holiday, Montana Box Set (Contains Books 1-5)

The Happy Ever After Series:
Flame and Ink
Ink Ever After

Single Title:
Finally Found You

**Next From NYT Bestselling Author Carrie Ann Ryan's
Dante's Circle Series**

It's odd how a strike of lightning can change a person's destiny, but it takes the decisions and strength of others to make it happen. The wind brushed against his wings and he brought them closer to his body, needing that ounce of control.

Ambrose Griffin looked out along the angelic enclave as he stood high on the cliff's edge and inhaled the fresh, open scent. This was his home, or at least it should have been. It was more of a resting place for him now. He didn't even know when the loss of home had come to him. Changes were coming, he felt them in every fiber of his being, yet he couldn't see their outcomes. To be honest, he really didn't want to. He might have been older than dirt, but he wasn't a seer. He didn't envy those who held that so-called gift.

Ambrose didn't want the world like it was. He'd seen countless civilizations rise and fall, people live and die faster than the sand that drifted away with their ashes along the wind.

Frankly, he was tired, the aches in his bones not from old age, but from time itself—he was an angel, he *didn't* age —but from the weight of his past.

He was a warrior angel. One designed, trained, and delegated to hand out the justice of the angelic council. His blade was the final cut of judgment. His sword was that of law and order. He lived and breathed the duties set forth by the council, the same council that beckoned him to join their ranks each time he saw them—at their request, not his.

Each time they summoned him and begged him to take a place within them, he'd declined. He'd seen the depravity of power and wanted nothing of it. The council had changed in the past year, a short time for an angel, but the change had been needed.

After the Angelic Wars—the centuries' long battles between two factions of angels—had ended, their council had been poisoned from within by Striker. The treasonous, brown-winged angel had started the Wars himself and had not stopped when the final blade had been lowered. No, he'd continued on in secret, almost killing Shade, Ambrose's brother-in-arms, and Shade's true-half, Lily.

They had persevered, and now Striker was no more— killed at the hands of Shade himself. Yet, with Striker's death, the empty seat on the council beckoned him, or rather the other council members had. He wanted nothing to do with it. He had all the power he wanted and desired nothing more. He didn't want to sit idly by and make declarations and decisions for others. No, he'd rather feel a blade warm in his hand as he fought for all that was right.

It was all he had done for his five-thousand-year existence and all he could see in his future. He needed nothing else.

Not even *her*.

No, it wasn't the time to think of her. It was never the time to think of her.

He'd seen the worst in man and angel alike far more often than not. Angels weren't the godly and holy beings people thought. Though those might exist—he wasn't so sure—they did not enter this realm or any of the other supernatural realms.

Humans weren't exactly as human as others would like to think. No, they were diluted versions of all things inhuman. Centuries of breeding with other supernaturals had created a supernatural without magic. Though, at first, the humans had known of magic and all it entailed, over time their true beginnings had been lost to them. Science and religion had warred with each other, erasing the true keystone to their humanity.

Now it was just as well. Humans weren't ready for the existences of angels, shifters, brownies, demons, and so many others to become common knowledge. They feared what they did not understand, and a war to end all wars would be an inevitable outcome. Seerers had foretold it, and Ambrose knew it to be truth deep down in his bones.

The gods, or whatever others called them, had other things in store however. A year before they'd struck seven women, seven close-knit friends, with a lightning strike that had unleashed the supernatural DNA within their genetic makeup. Each woman might or might not unleash the most prominent supernatural strain of DNA in their own code, though for their sakes, Ambrose hoped the latter. A change such as that would be a shock—no pun intended.

Lily, the first to change, had made it through and was now a brownie because of the lightning and the fact that she was stronger than she thought and had Shade by her side. Of course, it was also Shade's fault that her powers had been unearthed to begin with. Even with the lightning, it had taken their bonding and making love for her powers to be fully unleashed. A simple meeting with Shade had brought her powers to the surface, even though they had not been fully realized. It took that mating of a true half for the change to be complete.

It would be like that for the other six of them—if they met their true halves.

Any one of the other girls could be going through that pain that unsettled feeling that came with finding their true half but not completing the mating.

Ambrose gave a long sigh, one filled with an eternal memory that seemed to bear down on him with each passing day. With a swift intake of breath, he leapt off the edge of the cliff, his wings spreading wide, catching a wind current. He flew down to the ravine, following the river's path, the wind lashing through his hair. He never felt as alive as he did when he flew amongst the clouds and then again with nature. This was why he loved being an angel, even though the weight of the years felt heavier as time moved on.

He landed on the edge of a cliff that gave way to a marketplace. He'd told Shade and Lily he'd meet them on the other side of it, and he didn't want to be late. We walked past a grouping of younger female angels, and they each gave tentative smiles in his direction.

Well, they were younger to him. By the taste of their powers as they seeped off them, he knew them to be at least a few hundred years old. Babies to an ancient like him.

And if they were considered babies, then she—

No, he couldn't think about her. Not if he wanted to remain sane. He'd spent the past year in the angelic realm dealing with the aftermath of Striker's betrayal—away from her.

The girls—no, women—flexed their wings, each a painting of beauty and fragile elegance. Cool in their portrayal, iced in their immortally.

Not for him. No one was. Not even her.

Ambrose knew what the others saw. White wings, not as plain as those in the drawings by humans, but almost crystalline in nature, gleaming in the sunlight. He had the body of a warrior, one strengthened over eons of war and dispensing justice. His white hair ran straight down to the middle of his back, slightly mussed from his flight. He usually wore it tied back with a leather band but had opted to let it go free to feel like a younger man, a freer one.

What had he been thinking?

From the women's stares, he may have made a mistake. He didn't want their attention. He'd had his angel a lifetime ago and didn't want another. He knew what *could* be his fate, and the angels fluttering their eyelashes and wings were not it. He gave a regal nod and a cool stare. Their smiles vanished, but their gazes didn't waver.

Apparently, they liked the challenge?

No thanks. He didn't desire their attention, didn't deserve it. He was just a warrior angel, not a man to be admired.

He left them where they stood, their discontent clear, but he let it wash over him. The market was filled with the hustle and bustle of activity. Mothers held their babies close because a child was a prized gift in their culture. Children played in the street as there were no cars needed in their lands. Merchants sold goods as though it were a long-ago time in the human realm. The angels moved at a slower pace, though they held the technology to do anything. They were a mismatch of cultures and times. Some wore robes, while others, like him, wore jeans and other items of the modern movement.

He'd hated the robes anyway. The wind would always leave him feeling a bit breezy and exposed. He bit his lip to hold back a smile at the thought of what others would wear under those robes, didn't want to scare anyone today.

Ambrose walked past a group of young males play-fighting with wooden swords. Although a bullet could pierce a body, angelic or not, most angels preferred the more elegant weapon to fight, and for a warrior, it was a must. These young boys had their sights on the warrior class, one that would take much effort, but he'd help them when it came time for their mentoring—if they made it that far. Wordlessly, he walked up to one boy and adjusted the grip of his sword before moving on. He stopped abruptly when he noticed they were all frozen in place, their mouths open in shock.

"You need to be sure you handle your weapons with care," he advised, his voice deep and rough with lack of use. He only spoke if needed; there was no use in wasting words when actions would prove just as useful, if not more so. "Your opponent will be stronger than you in some cases, and you need to rely on your skill, as well as what's ingrained in you. Be aware."

With a nod, he left them in silence. Behind him, he heard murmurs of his name, whispers in reverence. He'd done that boy a favor, something the boy's father should have done. Though Ambrose was a warrior, he was also a mentor and a weapons enthusiast. Weapons were his passion.

His only passion these days.

His collection rivaled those of the best museums, if not surpassed them. Scholars would envy it had they known it existed, but his life was shrouded in secret from the humans, as it should be.

"Scaring young children, are you?" Shade Griffin said as he walked toward him with his arm around his true half and wife, Lily. Shade was his brother-in-arms, his partner in justice, brother by choice and not blood.

He was also the brother of his late wife, though that had been long ago.

Lily laughed, a sweet trill that made Ambrose think of family. She was now his sister, someone he'd die to protect, and her beauty surpassed most: ivory skin, large green eyes, and chestnut hair. He could easily see why Shade had fallen in love the moment he'd seen her.

"Shade, stop making fun of Ambrose," Lily scolded and elbowed him in the ribs.

"You still laughed, my dear," Shade said and kissed her temple.

She blushed and ducked her head. Ambrose lifted a corner of his lip and rubbed her cheek with his knuckle. Shade raised a brow, and Ambrose moved back, not caring in the slightest that Shade was territorial. He didn't fault the other angel for his attitude, but Shade should know Ambrose had another on his mind and didn't want Lily that way. It was still fun to needle him, even though the world thought he wasn't the most humorous of men.

"You're fine, Lily," he soothed. "I know you only laugh with him to humor him. He needs the help with his fragile ego."

Shade threw his head back and laughed. "Ambrose just told a joke and almost smiled." He clutched his chest and staggered back, bringing Lily with him. "I think I need to sit down."

"You're a riot, oh-wise-one," Ambrose said dryly. "Was there a reason you wanted to meet here?"

Lily looked around, her face radiant, glowing even. Was she…? Perhaps, but he'd let her tell him the news. Women seemed to like that.

"I've never been here before, so I thought it would be a nice change," Lily said, practically bouncing on her feet.

In the past year since their meeting, she'd been to the angelic realm a few times, but only to Shade's home or his own. She and Shade spent most of their time in the human realm, protecting her six friends in case the other supernaturals found out exactly what was going on and it turned dangerous. Ambrose had said he would help but had taken the coward's way out and gone back to the angels to help deal with Striker's betrayal.

He knew his break from the humans was almost at an end. The angels didn't need him anymore to oversee the change, and he knew the human women needed him more. Shade, and the girls' dragon friend, Dante, were on watch, but Ambrose should have helped more.

He still had time though. Maybe he could make amends.

"Ambrose?" Shade asked, worry in his features.

Ambrose shook away his thoughts and guilt and looked back to his two best friends. "Sorry, I was lost in thought. What is it you needed to tell me?"

Lily and Shade shared a worried glance that transformed to pure bliss, and a little stress on Shade's side.

"We're pregnant!" Lily explained, her cheeks rosy and her eyes bright.

Ambrose smiled, full out, a rarity, he knew. He pulled Lily into a tight hug and twirled her around. "Congratulations, Lily, my dear, you will be a wonderful mother."

Images of his own children's faces flashed in a fading memory, but he didn't feel any pain, only that hollowness of a long-lost future.

He put Lily down and gave her a chaste kiss on the mouth. "I will be there for you if you need me."

He clapped Shade on the back, and Shade gave him a look that said the other angel knew what Ambrose had been thinking about. They'd been friends and brothers too long to hide those things.

"I'm very happy for the both of you," Ambrose said. He pulled back and held his arm across his chest. "I will do all in my power to ensure your child, and your future children, are safe and happy," he vowed.

Shade mirrored his movement, and they both bowed. Tears stained Lily's cheeks, but she still held her smile.

"You'll be godfather, Ambrose, right?" she asked.

As if he could say no. He nodded, pleasure at the thought of their trust running through him.

"Of course," he said, his voice choked with emotion.

"We've already told the others in the human realm," Lily continued. "Sorry we didn't tell you first, but it didn't make any sense to come here before telling them."

"I don't mind, Lily."

"Jamie will be godmother; is that okay?" Lily asked. He knew she'd sensed something off between him and her friend, but thankfully, she hadn't broached the subject.

Jamie.

The name he'd fought so hard to forget.

The woman who haunted his dreams, more so than his dead wife.

Jamie, the woman who could have been his true half if he'd let it happen—who *was* his true half.

"Of course," he said again, this time a new emotion threatening to choke him. "Let's celebrate with a good meal, shall we?" He led them to a small eatery, his thoughts not on their conversation, but on the woman he'd avoided.

Jamie deserved more, a future. Not the broken shell of a man. He wasn't selfish enough to think he would make her happy, though he desperately wanted to be that man. Sometimes he thought he could be—could see their future.

No, he couldn't. She was too young for him. Too full of life. She'd be happier without him.

He closed his eyes while Shade and Lily talked to each other. He tugged on the cord that connected him and Jamie, the one she didn't know existed because she hadn't made the change to supernatural yet, even though he knew she was feeling the effects of the need to change. Luckily, it hadn't been as bad as Lily's, so he could leave her. She might feel only slightly weak, but she hadn't had the seizures or other side effects that Lily had endured, thankfully.

Unlike Lily though, Jamie had been feeling the weakness for almost a year.

And, it was his fault.

He'd left her, and they hadn't made love.

Hadn't even kissed.

He hadn't wanted to tie her to a man too old to be what she needed. In his heart, he'd known there was another for her. He'd felt it. The world consisted of just one true half per person, and some triads, Ambrose felt for certain there was another for Jamie, one that would be her true half. He knew in his heart that she would be happy with that other man, whoever he may be.

He sighed. Now he was just kidding himself. There wasn't potentially several mates out there for any one person. If he could feel like something was missing, like there was another for her, then that meant there had to be someone for him, as well.

He shook his head. No, he couldn't think about that.

Not yet.

Jamie was not the one for him, despite the cord that tethered them. Despite the lightning that had caused it all to begin with.

Her body was weakening because she'd met him and he'd started that change—or, in his opinion, that curse. He couldn't let her go through it any longer. No, he wouldn't be with her. She deserved better, but he *could* find that other man. The one he knew existed as sure as he felt the cord that connected him and Jamie. He would do what he must to find that man for her. He couldn't bear to think of her in any more pain.

Or any pain at all to think of it.

Nevertheless, he knew more pain was coming. She'd been living too easily for too long, and fate was a bitch when she wanted to be. Their connection might have allowed him to heal her physically, just like the night of Striker's death when he'd first felt the cord, but he couldn't heal this. He knew he would have to find this other man for her to be whole. That way she could find for her the one who could help her find her supernatural half and live in peace.

He would find him so Jaime could feel alive again.

Ambrose wasn't for her. No, he was for no one.

He wouldn't wallow, but he would live like he always had, hollow but with a purpose.

Jamie.

Pyro paced the length of his foyer, anger rolling through him with each step. His son was dying, but not fast enough for his taste. The bastard had forsaken their oaths and refused to take souls into the hells realm. Why couldn't the little twit die already?

Soon though, Pyro felt Balin begin to fade more with each day and relished it. Within days, Pyro wouldn't have to deal with the chain that shackled him to this realm. Although Balin didn't force him to remain in hell, if Pyro left, he was afraid of the damage Balin would do in his absence.

Like free the slaves and gladiators.

No, that wouldn't do.

Pyro went to his throne, an ornate chair made of the bones of his enemies, and plopped down, his body weary with boredom, something that could never do for a demon such as he.

He needed something to pass the time waiting for Balin to die. He couldn't kill his son in hell. No, ever since Lucifer had killed his own son in hell, they'd put a curse on the ability to kill one's loved ones. Damn that demon for ruining everything like always.

Maybe it was time to put his other plan in place. With Balin about to die, Pyro could use his men and powers to hurt the enemy who'd given him the scar that ran down the side of his body. The scar that revolted the women he took to his bed. Though they had to deal with it anyway, he wouldn't let them leave once he found them. That was not a demon's way.

Yes, it was time to pay Ambrose a visit.

He couldn't go to the angelic realm to find him. No, that would start a war, a war he would relish, but he was not in the mood to deal with the politics. However, he *could* go to the human realm and *not* start a war—it was in his blood. No one cared about the humans anyway. They were just the piss and backwater of the purebloods.

And, if his sources here correct, there was a woman who'd peaked the old angel's interest. A woman who'd been struck by lightning and lived to tell the tale. No, the two angels and that dragon where not as secretive as they thought. All of the realms knew something was amiss with those women, but no one cared enough to deal with it unless it affected them.

One of them had turned into a brownie.

He wondered what the woman who Ambrose had set his gaze on would turn into.

Maybe Pyro could cut it out of her.

Oh yes, that sounded like a plan. He'd take the girl and bring Ambrose to him. Though the angel wouldn't want an all-out war by stepping on hell's land, he could find a way to make it happen. The old bastard was crafty like that.

Pyro smiled, his teeth lengthening, his talons curling.

Yes, this would work. He'd send his men to get the girl, play with her to his heart's content, and the old winged bastard would come to him.

And, while all of this was happening, Balin would die from his own stubbornness, his own failure to do what was meant to be a demon.

Perfect.

A scream tore from the woman he'd pinned to the wall earlier and he sighed.

Fuck, he'd forgotten about her in all his planning. Well, it was of no use wasting a human since they were so hard to come by these days. Fools were forgetting the magic and not summoning the demons as often.

Pity to those who did.

Pyro took out his blade, sharp and deadly, just the right size of blade to extract the most pain and smiled again. He stood then walked to his captive.

"You really should know not to summon things stronger than you," he warned as he slowly sliced away at her flesh. The human's eyes turned a brassy dull, the life fading out of her as she screamed, and he let the terror wash over him in pure bliss.

"Sadly, I'm bored with you now, so I'm going to give you to my men. I was going to kill you, but now I have another human in mind."

Her blood spattered on his bare arms and he turned away, licking the rivulets as he did so. With a nod to his men who had come into the room at the final scream, two of them went to her, grins on their faces.

Pyro had to find this human woman and lure Ambrose to him. That was his goal. The other humans could wait until later. A scream filled with insurmountable pain echoed along the walls behind him, and he took a deep breath, letting the horror seep into his pores.

It would be a good day.

Finally, Ambrose would pay.

Find out more in <u>Her Warriors' Three Wishes</u>. Out Now. To make sure you're up to date on all of Carrie Ann's releases, sign up for her mailing list <u>HERE</u>.